Princess Esofi of Rhodia and Crown Prince Albion of Ieflaria have been betrothed since they were children but have never met. At age seventeen, Esofi's journey to Ieflaria is not for the wedding she always expected but instead to offer condolences on the death of her would-be husband.

But Ieflaria is desperately in need of help from Rhodia for their dragon problem, so Esofi is offered a new betrothal to Prince Albion's younger sister, the new Crown Princess Adale. But Adale has no plans of taking the throne, leaving Esofi with more to battle than fire-breathing beasts.

THE QUEEN OF

IEFLARIA

Tales of Inthya, Book One

Effie Calvin

A NineStar Press Publication

Published by NineStar Press
P.O. Box 91792,
Albuquerque, New Mexico, 87199 USA.
www.ninestarpress.com

The Queen of Ieflaria

Printed in the USA
Second Edition
July, 2019

Print ISBN: 978-1-951057-22-0

Also available in eBook, ISBN: 978-1-948608-05-3

This book is dedicated to my cat, Dottie, because I am an unironic lesbian stereotype.

A very special thank-you to all my beta readers who helped me out along the way!

Chapter One

ESOFI

The castle at Birsgen had been built from cold gray stone, but the rooms within were warm and bright. Intricate tapestries and carpets in rich shades of crimson, emerald, and sapphire decorated the throne room, and a roaring fire at the far end of the room kept the worst of the chill that dwelled in the ancient stone at bay.

Princess Esofi of Rhodia sank into a curtsy, her elaborate skirts rustling softly in the silence. Before her were the velvet thrones of King Dietrich and Queen Saski of Ieflaria. Just behind her were the waiting ladies and battlemages who had accompanied her on the four-month journey to a land that would be her new home.

With Esofi's entire retinue crowded inside, the throne room was not nearly as expansive as it ought to be. To make things even more uncomfortable, many of the residents of the Ieflarian court had gathered for the arrival of the princess, filling the room further.

Most of the Ieflarians Esofi had seen so far were dark-haired and fair-skinned with eyes of blue or gray, though in the larger cities she had encountered people who were clearly from far-off lands like Anora and Masim. The women usually wore their hair in braids, with younger girls allowing them to hang free and older women pinning them into coronets or coils. Esofi wished that she could take in their faces and study their reactions to her presence. But she knew she had to trust her ladies to do that for her while she devoted her attention to the regents.

"We welcome you to Ieflaria during this sad time," said King Dietrich. "We regret that your arrival has been under such unfortunate circumstances."

Esofi swallowed. Every Ieflarian they'd encountered since coming into the country had been dressed in gray or black or somber lavender. The queen herself was in a plain gray gown with only the simplest pearl circlet on her head, and the king wore a black velvet jacket over a gray tunic and breeches. Even the guards and servants wore black, instead of the crimson-and-gold livery that her books and tutors had told her to expect.

Esofi had worn her simplest dress out of respect, and her ladies had done the same. But Rhodian fashion was dramatically more opulent than the clothing found in Ieflaria, featuring lace accessories, layers of ruffled underskirts, and fabrics sewn with gemstones. Even the most subdued ensemble seemed disrespectfully lavish compared to the simple styles favored by the Ieflarians.

"Yes," said Esofi. "I am deeply sorry."

Three months. Crown Prince Albion, Esofi's husband-to-be and heir to the throne of Ieflaria, had been dead for three months. Esofi had never met him, but they'd been exchanging letters since they were old enough to write. The loss still felt unreal, as though it were all a terrible joke.

"We are no longer able to uphold the contract that was signed fifteen years ago," said Queen Saski. "You have the right to return home if you choose."

She was wrong. Esofi could no more return home than she could transform into a bird and fly away.

"Your Majesties," Esofi said. "Your lands have suffered greatly from dragon attacks in past years and will only continue to suffer if action is not taken. As the future queen, it was my intention to begin securing Ieflaria's borders immediately. To this end, I have brought with me a company of the finest battlemages that the University of Rho Dianae has to offer." She gestured to the back of the room where fifty mages stood in the midnight-blue robes that marked them as fully trained battlemages blessed by Talcia, Goddess of Magic. "But I believe this can still be accomplished, even now. I remain willing to marry your heir... your new heir."

King Dietrich and Queen Saski both looked relieved, as if they had expected Esofi to pick up her skirts and flounce all the way back to Rho Dianae.

"For the sake of honoring the spirit of our agreement and protecting our homeland," said King Dietrich, "we are willing to grant you this."

Even though it had been her proposal, Esofi felt a soft pang in her heart at the words. Albion would have been gentle. Albion would have been kind. She had always considered herself lucky that her betrothed seemed to be noble in manner as well as blood and so near to her own age. Esofi had seen enough violent lords and vicious ladies to know that Iolar had smiled upon her when her parents had arranged her fate.

"Thank you, Your Majesty," said Esofi. "I think my parents would have little reason to object if the terms of the marriage were otherwise unchanged."

"Then in three days, we will formalize the new agreement." King Dietrich gestured to a servant who came hurrying to his side. Esofi could not hear what the king said to him, but the servant rushed from the room immediately.

Esofi tried to remember who exactly the heir to Ieflaria's throne was now that Albion was gone. Surely, someone had told her at some point. The winged courier who had brought the news of Albion's death might have mentioned it. But Esofi's grief-stricken mind offered no names. Her gaze found the statue of Iolar, Fourth of the Ten, where it loomed behind Their Majesties' thrones. She offered up a rapid prayer to him.

"We have prepared rooms for you," said Queen Saski. "The servants will lead you to them. If they are not to your liking, you may arrange them however you wish." Her smile was warm and possibly even genuine.

"Thank you," said Esofi with another curtsy. "The journey has been long. It will be good to rest in a proper bed again."

"You will have plenty of time to recover from your journey," said Queen Saski. "We cannot begin wedding arrangements until one hundred days of mourning have passed. Tomorrow, you will join me for tea and meet my daughter, the Crown Princess Adale."

"Of course, Your Majesty," began Esofi. "I..." But the rest of her words died in her throat as her mind caught up with her ears. Princess Adale. She had heard that name before. She was Albion's younger sister and the only other child of King Dietrich and Queen Saski. Albion had mentioned her in his letters, spinning tales of their adventures and mischief.

But...a princess? Like most people, Esofi did not have a strong preference regarding the gender of the one she married. But marrying the same sex was a privilege that royalty was seldom able to indulge in, since the production of heirs usually took priority over all else. Two women could still manage it if one of them could hold a

Changed shape long enough, but men had to be content with surrogates. Most of the nobility back home did not care to take such risks with their bloodlines. Perhaps it was different in Ieflaria. Or perhaps Their Majesties were merely desperate.

Fortunately, Queen Gaelle of Rhodia had instilled iron willpower in her children, and so Esofi was able to successfully fight back her urge to turn around and look to her ladies for their reactions. She realized the king and queen were still waiting for her to finish her sentence.

"I...think that will be lovely," she completed. Then she pressed the back of her hand to her forehead as delicately as she could manage. "Goodness, how the journey has wearied me."

"Then go, rest," said Queen Saski. "We will speak again tomorrow."

Dismissed at last, Esofi gave one last curtsy before turning and leading the procession from the room. Once they were out in the halls, Captain Henris approached her. He wore the same midnight robes as the other battlemages, but his were trimmed in silver embroidery. Captain Henris was not a young man any longer but had served Esofi well during the long journey, and she found that she trusted him implicitly.

"Your orders, Princess?" he asked.

"You may send the mages to the barracks," Esofi said. "Tell them that I thank them for their service. And find me tomorrow morning, before I meet with Her Majesty."

"Of course, Princess," he said.

With the departure of the mages, the hall became significantly less crowded. Esofi turned her attention to her ladies. There were three of them, and all had come with her by choice. The first was Lady Lexandrie, the second daughter of the Duke and Duchess of Fialia and Esofi's second cousin, who had been her waiting lady since they were thirteen. She was a tall woman with a cascade of golden hair and a regal demeanor. If Lexandrie had any faults, the foremost one was stubbornness, followed closely by an innate belief that no person in the world had ever worked as hard or suffered as desperately as she had in her eighteen years of life at the marble palace of Rho Dianae.

Next was Lady Mireille, daughter of the Baron and Baroness of Aelora. With six older siblings, her prospects in Rhodia had not been high—but her ambitions were. Esofi was still not entirely certain how the young woman had managed to win herself a place on the royal procession, but that didn't matter now. Mireille's traveling papers had proclaimed that she was sixteen years old, but her youthful face could have passed for twelve.

Mireille's presence had been welcome on the long journey. She was a bright, cheerful young woman, desperately eager to please and only occasionally prone to simpering. She would rush eagerly to complete any task Esofi set them to, and Lexandrie was always happy to let her work in solitude until the assignment was minutes from being complete.

In some small way, Esofi felt that she and Mireille had a sort of kinship between them. While Lexandrie was certain to return to Rhodia someday, Mireille and Esofi never would. There was nothing left for them back there. Ieflaria would become their world now.

And last was Lady Lisette of Diativa, who was in actuality not a Lady, nor of Diativa, nor even named Lisette. She was a tiny woman with black eyes and hair the color of moonlight who could go days at a time without uttering a word. Esofi did not know for certain how many blades, lockpicks, and poisons Lisette had on her person, but she felt quite sure that the number was absurdly high. She was an unnerving girl until one became accustomed to her, but Esofi's mother had insisted upon her presence in the royal carriage.

"Such a lovely welcome," said Lexandrie in a bright and vapid tone. "Didn't you think so, Princess?"

"Yes, of course," said Esofi in an equally cheerful tone—she knew perfectly well that there could be any number of people listening in, waiting for some word against the co-regents or a sign of weakness. The fact that they spoke in the language of Rhodia was no protection against that. "I will be glad to rest my feet at last, though, and for a cup of tea."

"Princess Esofi," said a woman, emerging from the throne room behind them. She looked to be around the same age as Queen Saski and wore a lavender gown decorated with pearls. In keeping with the Ieflarian fashion, her long hair was in coiled braids. "I am Countess Amala of Eiben, waiting lady to Queen Saski. Her Majesty has asked me to show you to your new rooms."

"Oh! Of course," said Esofi, stepping aside so Amala could take the lead.

Amala walked down the lamp-lit hallway with rapid, purposeful footsteps, speaking candidly as she went, naming each room as they passed it. Esofi glanced back at her ladies, and Lisette had a particularly intense expression upon her face. Esofi knew she could trust her to remember everything they were being told and was glad for her presence.

They continued through a maze of stone halls, servants and nobility alike stepping aside to stare at the foreigners in their castle. Esofi kept a practiced smile at her lips the entire time, until finally Amala came to a stop in front of a large door, ornately carved with a depiction of a unicorn in a meadow.

Amala withdrew a key from the purse at her belt and unlocked the door. "These will be your rooms, Princess. You will find adjoining rooms for your ladies, and Her Majesty has already assigned servants to see to your needs."

Amala gestured to her, and Esofi stepped inside. The first room was an elaborate parlor, furnished in the Ieflarian style, all intricately carved dark woods and jewel-toned carpets and tapestries. Glass oil lamps cast the room in a golden glow, and a small fire burned in the stone hearth.

At the center of the room stood a middle-aged woman, large-boned and silver-haired with a nose like an eagle's beak. She wore the uniform of the castle staff, but Esofi could tell from just a moment's glance that the woman was not a maid.

"Mistress Abbing is the palace housekeeper," explained Amala, and the woman curtsied. Esofi nodded at her.

"If there is anything you require, Princess," said Mistress Abbing, "tell any of my girls. If you catch them lazing about, send them directly to me and I'll sort them out. We'll come in to clean once a week while you're at the sunrise service."

Esofi nodded again. There was never a day that the Temple of Iolar did not perform a sunrise service or the corresponding sundown service in the evening. But most people only attended on the first day of the week. In some circles, that first service was considered mandatory.

"That room will be yours, Princess," Amala explained, gesturing to a door on one side of the room. "You will find the servants are already unpacking your things. They should be gone within the hour. And for your ladies, their rooms are through that other door. If there is anything you require, Her Majesty has ordered it will be given to you."

And with that, Amala excused herself. Mistress Abbing went into Esofi's room to yell at the servants, and Esofi immediately sank down onto the nearest sofa, only to pause in wonderment at the softness—after three months at sea and another in a carriage, she had almost forgotten what proper furniture felt like.

"Well—" began Lexandrie, only to be cut off by Lisette raising one thin, pale finger into the air.

"Not yet," said Lisette, and embarked on a rapid search of the entire room. Esofi sat very still as Lisette examined everything and anything, turning over cushions and pulling books off the shelves and even tapping at the stones on the walls. After a few moments, Lisette seemed satisfied.

"Nothing in here, at least," she said.

"May I speak now, then?" asked Lexandrie. Then, without waiting for a reply, she went on. "Esofi, have you realized—?"

"That they mean for me to marry Princess Adale? Yes," said Esofi.

"And you will agree to it?"

"It makes no difference to me, does it?" asked Esofi. "I shall marry someone at the end of the mourning period. Or would you have me return home and tell my parents that I rejected the heir to the throne of Ieflaria?"

"Of course not," said Lexandrie. "But you're not a peasant. You need heirs. And I *know* you can't hold on to a Changed body long enough to—"

"But maybe the Crown Princess Adale can!" interrupted Mireille.

"Perhaps she can," Esofi agreed. "Or perhaps there is a sizable list of heirs already, and so Their Majesties are not concerned. Until I speak with Queen Saski tomorrow, we will not know, and I will not spend any more time worrying about it, not while there's a fresh bed and a warm fire waiting in the next room."

Fortunately, none of her ladies seemed to be in the mood to argue, and the four sat in exhausted silence until the servants were herded out by Mistress Abbing, who bid them a good night and reminded them to only ask if they required something, no matter the hour.

The ladies went into Esofi's room, which was furnished in a similar fashion to the outer parlor. It featured an area with a bookcase and writing desk, and a table set with a bowl of unfamiliar fruit, which Lisette ordered them all not to touch. The far wall had a large window that overlooked the dusky gardens.

Esofi's ladies set to the task of unlacing her complicated dress and corsets. After some brief but frantic searching, Mireille found her nightgowns in the dresser.

Once in bed, Esofi tried to keep her thoughts clear of speculation, but it was easier said than done. She turned her thoughts to the gods, as she had been instructed in her childhood.

There were as many gods in Asterium as there were stars in the sky, though Esofi only really concerned herself with the Ten. She wondered if Iolar was watching her from Solarium but immediately dismissed the thought as hubris. As a princess, she knew she fell solidly into his domain, but she had never felt that deep spiritual connection with the father of all Men that she ought to.

Perhaps Talcia was watching instead from her home in Dia Asteria? Perhaps. But it seemed infinitely more likely that she was being casually observed by some extremely specific minor deity from a tiny pocket of Asterium that nobody had even heard of before.

Each god, no matter how minor, had a place in Asterium where they brought their beloved followers after their deaths. The sole exception to this was Eran, God of Dreams, who brought the living into Ivoria on an almost nightly basis.

Esofi knew that her own deceased family members were almost certainly with Talcia. She wondered where Albion was. Solarium, most likely, surrounded by some of the bravest and wisest regents that Inthya had ever known, where they would discuss and debate into eternity.

The thought made her heart ache.

Esofi was weary from the journey, and the sheets had been warmed by heated stones placed by thoughtful servants. She fell asleep quickly, and if she was invited into Ivoria that night, she did not remember it when she awoke.

THE NEXT MORNING, Esofi opened her eyes and gave a little start at the sight of the unfamiliar stone ceiling above her head. It took her a moment to remember where she was. Ieflaria. Birsgen. The castle. Queen Saski would be summoning her that day.

At the thought, Esofi sat bolt upright and leapt from bed. Hurrying over to the nearest wardrobe, Esofi was greeted by the sight of a host of barely familiar dresses. She had forgotten just how many she'd commissioned and packed away before leaving home, with the strict orders that they be left untouched for the entire journey.

Unfortunately, none were suitable for mourning. Esofi knew that she was not expected to partake in the mourning period, being a foreigner, but felt that a too-grandiose display would seem insensitive, especially since Albion had been her betrothed.

The day before, all of the Ieflarian ladies had been dressed in simple but elegant gowns with skirts that fell naturally from the underbust. It was a stark contrast to the voluminous and many-layered dresses that were popular in Rhodia. Perhaps she could have some Ieflarian dresses made up for her.

Esofi sorted through the dresses, trying to pick the most subdued one. It was not long before there was a knock at her door.

"Enter," called Esofi, and Lexandrie and Mireille hurried in. They were in their long, lacy nightdresses.

"We thought we heard you up," explained Mireille. "Why did you not call us?"

"I only just woke." Esofi did not turn away from her wardrobe. "Is Lisette gone?"

"Of course," said Lexandrie, a bit of annoyance in her tone. "There's work to be done, so naturally she's missing."

"That is to be expected," murmured Esofi. "Her assignment here is different than ours, after all."

"Still—" Lexandrie seemed to be trying not to let her annoyance show now that the princess had made her position clear. "She could at least try to act like a proper waiting lady."

Esofi selected a gown of palest pink decorated with buttercream ruffles and little silk rosebuds. Her ladies helped her dress, lacing her into her corsets and lifting layer after layer of fabric over Esofi's head until finally the dress looked suitable.

While Mireille pressed Esofi's blonde hair into curls with a hot iron, Lexandrie set to the task of applying the princess's powder and rouge. Once that was finished, they pinned silk flowers in her hair and stood back to admire their handiwork.

"It's not too much, is it?" worried Esofi as Mireille retrieved a porcelain hand mirror.

"Too much?" Lexandrie had a touch of incredulity in her voice. "You're meeting with the queen. There is no such thing as too much!" She cast a wistful look back at Esofi's closet, her gaze settling on an elaborate crimson-and-gold gown. Esofi chose to ignore this.

Lexandrie and Mireille left to prepare themselves for the day, and Esofi found her embroidery bag inside her bedside table after a few minutes of searching. She wished she could have overseen the servants as they unpacked. It would probably take a great deal of effort to arrange everything the way that she liked it.

Esofi went into the parlor and was surprised by multiple baskets and packages waiting for her on the table. Pinned to the largest basket was a hastily scrawled note from Lisette.

> *Princess,*
>
> *The packages are all safe to handle. I know you would have liked to open them yourself, but it was better this way. I didn't detect anything amiss,*

but I wouldn't be displeased if you threw it all out anyway, especially the food.

Lisette

Esofi reached for the nearest basket and pulled out the card, which named an Ieflarian noble that she had never heard of as the benefactor. The other gifts were much the same, each bearing a card with an unfamiliar name and title. Not all were nobles, though. A canvas painting of the royal chase had been sent from the court painter, and the parcel from the Lacemaker's Guild contained a pair of gloves, dyed lavender. There was also a bottle of wine from the Vesoldan Ambassador.

Esofi decided it would be more fun to explore the gifts if her ladies were there with her. She went over to open the window and let the cool morning sunlight in, and then sat herself on the sofa. During the journey, they had spent endless hours embroidering in the carriage while practicing their Ieflarian conversation. So great was the association in Esofi's mind that she found herself murmuring verb conjugations as she took a pair of silver scissors from her bag and carefully cut out the awkward, crooked stitching from the corner of the tablecloth that had been Lisette's responsibility.

Esofi had been betrothed to Albion at the age of three, and so much of her education had focused on the fact that she would someday become the queen of Ieflaria. Along with the ordinary tutor who had educated her entire family, Queen Gaelle had also hired an Ieflarian tutor especially for Esofi. He had taught her the nation's history and language, and Esofi was confident that she knew as much about Ieflarian history and economics as she did about Rhodia's, or at least as much as could be put into books.

Still, none of the reading she had done had prepared her for the beautiful sweeping farmlands that made up the majority of the Ieflarian countryside. She would never forget the first time she had laid eyes upon the land that stretched as far as the eye could see, hills beyond hills and fields beyond fields. In that moment, she could have believed that it all went on forever.

It was still early spring, and from her carriage window she had been able to watch the farmers at work, tilling the ebony soil in strict, even rows. The ones who were blessed by Eyvindr, God of the Harvest, had performed the rituals that would sink green magic into the earth and ensure a good harvest. Meanwhile, shepherds and milkmaids drove their animals to grassy green fields, stopping at shrines to Cyne to mutter prayers or leave small offerings or simply run their hands across the stones.

In Ieflaria, and indeed on the entire continent of Ioshora, Cyne was the Eleventh. The Eleventh was the god that served as a tiebreaker to the Ten, the most powerful gods in Asterium. The Ten were the same all the world over (or at least, all the parts of the world Esofi had read about), but the Eleventh differed across regions.

Back home in Rhodia, the Eleventh had been Nara, Goddess of the Sky. But here, with farmlands taking up so much of the geography, she could understand how Cyne, the God of Animals and son of Eyvindr, had become more powerful.

Overlooking the farms were always a few soldiers or, if the town was particularly fortunate, paladins from the Order of the Sun. Their attention would be not on the land but the skies above, ready to sound the alarm at the first sound of heavy wingbeats. Their presence was a grim reminder of the constant danger that hovered overhead.

Esofi's understanding of the dragon situation was thus: At the height of its power, nearly a millennium ago, the Xytan Empire had driven every last dragon from the continent. The dragons had retreated to a small cluster of unclaimed islands that lay between the northeastern coast of modern-day Ieflaria and the southeastern coast of Veravin. From that day forward, they only occasionally troubled the lands of Men.

But centuries passed, and the Xytan Empire began to crumble. One by one, its outermost territories rallied their own armies and declared independence. Ieflaria's own independence was a relatively bloodless transition, as most of the Xytan soldiers were well aware they were outmatched and chose to retreat home.

Under the new regime, the dragon attacks remained infrequent enough to be regarded nearer to legends than threats. Things had only started to change in the last few decades, when the strikes had grown in frequency.

Esofi had not realized anything was truly amiss until one day, about five years past, when Albion wrote to her that the dragons were no longer coming to Ieflaria simply to steal cattle. They had started burning towns and attacking soldiers all along the coastline. Esofi wrote back that she was sure the Ieflarian military could handle the problem, and suggested a hope that the attacks would die down once the dragons learned that venturing into Ieflaria would end badly.

But it seemed that things had only become worse in the interim years.

Esofi had met refugees during her journey to the capital. They were mostly from small coastal holdings, fishing towns that had been destroyed in a matter of moments. The refugees had traveled inland, seeking the protection of their lords. But these Ieflarians were unaccustomed to farm life and frequently expressed their desire to return to the seaside as soon as possible. Unfortunately for them, the nobility was refusing to rebuild until the danger had been dealt with.

Esofi could see both sides of the issue. There was no sense in expending the resources to rebuild a town only to see it destroyed again. But crowding refugees into small farming communities or minor southern cities was not a viable long-term solution either.

Despite their misfortunes, it did not seem that the Ieflarian people were using the death of the crown prince or the threat of dragon attacks as an excuse to forsake their work. They had been working in the fields or caring for their animals as Esofi's carriage passed by along her journey. Sometimes, they had raised their heads, their mild curiosity turning to fevered excitement when they caught a glimpse of blonde curls instead of ebony braids.

Esofi had been afraid that the people of Ieflaria would have no interest in her, the foreign bride rendered useless by the loss of her groom. But they still turned out to line the streets whenever she passed through, even in the smallest farming communities. Children had given her messy bouquets of wildflowers and called her Solviga, the Ieflarian name that sounded closest to her own. Old grandparents had clasped her hands (something shockingly disrespectful in Rhodia, but apparently as common as rain in Ieflaria) and prayed with her.

"She's so beautiful. They'll find someone to marry her in no time," the Ieflarians had proclaimed to one another when they knew Esofi was in earshot. "No need for her to turn around and go back home—that would be a tragedy, would it not?"

Their motives had been transparent but no less heartwarming.

The outer door opened, returning Esofi to the present. She set down her embroidery as Lisette slipped inside like a cat or perhaps the shadow of a cat. When she saw Esofi sitting there, she froze momentarily.

"Lady Lisette," greeted Esofi in a neutral tone. "I trust you are well."

Lisette said nothing. She never seemed to know exactly how to reply to pleasantries.

"Have you anything to report?" asked Esofi.

"Only gossip and speculation," said Lisette in that dry voice of hers. She crossed her arms. "But if you are truly able to handle the dragons, I think they will have little reason to complain."

"You know perfectly well that I can," said Esofi, focusing on her embroidery. "What else have they been saying?"

"There is also the question of heirs," said Lisette. "The Ieflarians worry that neither of you will be able to hold a Change long enough to produce one."

"Mm," said Esofi. "Well, we shall handle that situation when it arises. And what do they say of the Crown Princess Adale?"

"It would seem Her Highness is ill-suited to be her parents' heir or anyone's betrothed." Lisette's eyes narrowed. "She spends her days hunting, riding, or drinking, disrespects the gods, and takes no interest in state matters."

Esofi pressed her lips together.

"But," added Lisette with a touch of reluctance in her voice, "it seems the castle staff is genuinely fond of her. Several servants tried to convince me that she is of good character."

"Has she said anything of me?" asked Esofi.

"A servant was sent to her with the news yesterday," explained Lisette. "But he says she may have been too drunk to understand the message."

Esofi found herself wondering which purse her prayer beads were in. "Very well. Thank you for your service."

Lisette disappeared into the ladies' suite, and Esofi went on embroidering, admiring the way her hands did not tremble.

Next to arrive was Captain Henris. He was dressed in his familiar formal battlemage attire, and Esofi called for Mireille and Lexandrie to attend her for the meeting.

"The Ieflarian military is requesting we station our battlemages at every port, city, and town," he reported. "And they are eager to ship them out as quickly as possible."

Beside her, Lexandrie clicked her teeth together in agitation, and Esofi knew why. Ieflaria was a large country, and the plan struck her as overly ambitious. "We haven't enough mages for that. They would be spread too thinly."

"I fear the same," said Captain Henris. "The Ieflarians are overly excited at the prospect of easier victories against the dragons. I have explained to them that sending only one mage will do little good in most circumstances, but I feel they do not believe me. These Ieflarians are so unfamiliar with Talcia's magic, they earnestly believe a single ordinary battlemage can take down a dragon."

"If we order only a single battlemage to defend an entire holding, we are sentencing them to death the moment a dragon arrives," said Esofi. "I will not throw away their lives like that. But I will speak to Her Majesty today, and perhaps I can persuade her."

Captain Henris nodded. "I trust that you can. And will you tell her your plans for the university?"

"Yes," said Esofi. "And more of those battlemages will be needed here to teach what I cannot. Their Majesties' generals will not like it, but hopefully, they will come to see that a slower solution will protect us for generations to come."

"I believe in your tongue, Princess," said Henris, managing to coax a smile from Esofi. "Are you well otherwise?"

"Of course," said Esofi. "Our rooms are adequate, and we've come upon no great trouble so far. I look forward to meeting the crown princess today."

"Ah," said Henris. "Hm. Yes."

Esofi had a feeling that he'd heard the same stories that Lisette had, but merely smiled pleasantly. "If that is all, Captain?"

Henris bowed and showed himself out. Esofi allowed herself a little sigh and settled back onto the couch.

"Mireille, I would like to check the Ieflarian peerage again," she said. Mireille was up like an arrow loosed from a bow and returned quickly with a parchment folio. Esofi accepted it and flipped open to the page of the royal family tree.

She felt a soft little pang when her gaze fell upon Albion's name, but quickly forced her attentions elsewhere. There, beside him, was the name Adalheidis Verheicht.

She also knew that the crown passed through Dietrich's side of the family, and checked his siblings. He had a younger brother, Prince Radulfr, who was married to a Duchess Theudelinda and therefore not a marriageable candidate. They had two children, who were—Esofi did some quick counting—third and fourth in line for the throne, assuming nobody else had died in the last few months. She supposed that she ought to set her sights on them, if the crown princess turned out to be serious about abandoning her responsibilities.

But Esofi knew little of romance except what she had heard in stories and seen firsthand at Rho Dianae. She had been grateful for her arrangement with Albion, because it meant that she wouldn't have to play those confusing games that everyone at court was so fond of. She had never understood people who bemoaned marriage contracts that they'd had no say in. To Esofi's practical mind, marriage contracts represented certainty and security.

What chance did she have without one? Esofi knew she couldn't compete with the tall and elegant nobles of the Ieflarian court who would all have their attention on the throne now that Albion was gone. The thought filled her with dread. Esofi knew how to run a household, how to plan a defense, how to secure an alliance. But she did not know how to *beguile*. No, she would need a contract to be drawn up and signed immediately.

A servant arrived to escort them to breakfast. Esofi was still becoming accustomed to the large and heavy breakfasts that the Ieflarians preferred, and felt a little queasy when she sat down at the table and saw the rich meats and strangely prepared eggs that had been spread out across it. Back home in Rhodia, people ate little in the morning beyond a light piece of fruit or a small pastry.

Breakfast passed without incident, and eventually, Their Majesties dismissed everyone. With nothing else to do but await the queen's summons, Esofi returned to her rooms and decided to see if she could try to rearrange her things more to her taste.

She found her marble statuette of Talcia tucked away in one of the drawers, wrapped in the blue square of velvet that served as Esofi's altar cloth. Esofi immediately set both out on a table by the window. Her prayer beads and books quickly joined the display.

Talcia, Fifth of the Ten, was the Goddess of Magic. But she seemed to be less popular in Ieflaria than she was in Rhodia. Esofi had seen no shrines or temples to her since they'd come into the country. Perhaps that was why Ieflaria was so lacking in battlemages. Their blessing came from her, after all.

Talcia was also the wife of Iolar, the God of Law and Civilization to whom all regents looked for guidance. Together, they represented the duality of the known and unknown, fine ideals versus unpredictable reality.

If Esofi was allowed to set up her university, she would dedicate it to Talcia. Perhaps that would cause the goddess's attention to finally turn back to Ieflaria. It would take some time, but once Talcia began granting her magic to the Ieflarians, they would be able to hold their own against the dragons.

Esofi looked out the window at the gardens below. If she was lucky, she might be able to find some night-blooming flowers to leave as a fresh offering at her small altar. Of course, there was also the large offering she planned to make at the Great Temple of Iolar in gratitude for their safe journey, but that was more of a business transaction, akin to the large sum she had paid to the Mer for their protection when she sailed from Rho Dianae to Gennelet. Iolar was the patron of regents and lawmakers everywhere, and so Esofi knew she must make the appropriate offerings to him. But Esofi's family had always been closer to Talcia.

If she hadn't been waiting on Queen Saski's invitation, Esofi might have gone in search of the chapel right then. She had always felt comforted in temples, so near to the gods.

Queen Saski's summons came soon enough, though, delivered by Countess Amala herself. Esofi regretted that the invitation was for her alone. She would have liked to have her ladies nearby to assess Crown Princess Adale for themselves, though logic told her that Lisette would be in the garden somewhere.

Amala linked their elbows together in a shockingly familiar gesture—apparently the people of Ieflaria saw no shame in touching one another—as she led Esofi into the gardens. It was a lovely, bright day with the sun warming the grass and colorful springtime flowers in bloom. Gardeners were at work quietly, their fingertips occasionally shimmering with the green magic of Eyvindr as they coaxed open blossoms and rejuvenated dying plants.

Out on the grass, under a cloth pavilion, a table had been set for three. Queen Saski was already seated, talking to a servant. Esofi curtsied as she approached, and Saski smiled brightly.

"Sit, my dear," she said, gesturing to the chair nearest to herself. Esofi passed her parasol to the servant and began the careful process of seating herself without harming her dress.

"I am sorry to say my daughter has yet to show herself today," confided Queen Saski with a deep sigh. "I hope you do not take offense. She is... she has been having a bit of a difficult time since..."

"I understand," said Esofi.

"Still, I expect her to make an appearance soon." Queen Saski looked distinctly unhappy. "Perhaps you can tame her. Iolar knows I can't."

A servant filled Esofi's teacup.

"I hope your journey here wasn't too unpleasant," Saski continued. "The dragons... they are a pestilence. Many of our couriers have left the country altogether, and the few that still consent to fly charge exorbitant prices."

The couriers were operated by the Temple of Nara, and their blessing was one of the most enviable in all the world. Each had been born with a pair of enormous feathered wings emerging from their shoulder blades, large and powerful enough to allow flight. Couriers traveled across entire continents, carrying messages and enjoying unparalleled freedom. But despite their blessing, they were still Men, and stood little chance against a dragon. Esofi could not blame them for leaving.

"The dragons troubled our traveling caravan at first," Esofi said. "I believe it is because they smelled my dowry. But we drove them back—it was not difficult, with so many battlemages."

"So I have heard," said Saski, her face lighting with a smile. "I cannot tell you what it has meant to our people to see your mages fighting against the dragons and winning so easily. We have had such tales from the south these past weeks."

Esofi laughed. "I am sure most of them are wild exaggerations."

"Maybe so, but if it gives my subjects hope, I will not ask you to correct them," Saski said. Then she sighed. "I think this year alone has been worse than the past four combined. If this issue is not resolved soon, our people will begin to panic. The Order of the Sun does have a strong presence here, but their magic is primarily defensive. The battlemages you brought us will make all the difference, I am certain."

"Regarding the battlemages," said Esofi. "I wonder if I might make a proposal to you? I have had much time to think during the journey, and I believe I've come up with an idea that will protect us for many generations to come."

But Queen Saski never had the chance to respond, because that was when a long shadow fell across the table and the Crown Princess Adale decided to put in an appearance.

Adale was a tall, lanky woman with an oval face and a thin nose. She wore her long, dark hair in a pair of braids that had been allowed to swing free, rather than being pinned up. Here and there, curls had escaped to cradle her face or occasionally stick straight up in the air. She was dressed in what had once been a lovely silver gown in the Ieflarian style but now was covered in grass stains.

Esofi's fingers gave an involuntary little twitch. She'd left her prayer beads in her room.

"Adale!" Queen Saski sounded more exhausted than scandalized. "Where have you been? We've been waiting—"

"I'm here now, aren't I?" retorted Adale.

Esofi rose from her seat abruptly and sank into a formal curtsy. "My lady, I am pleased to meet you at last."

Adale did not respond immediately. She seemed to be at a loss. Then she slouched into a chair and pulled a tray of sandwiches toward herself. Esofi returned to her seat at a more sedate pace, wondering if it would be most advantageous to turn the conversation back to her proposal for the university or attempt to engage with Adale.

"Where have you been this morning, Adale?" asked Queen Saski.

Adale answered with a shrug.

"It must have been important, since you kept your new bride waiting for nearly half an hour."

"I thought I'd give her a chance to run away," said Adale.

Saski snatched the sandwich from her daughter's hand. "Can you be serious for a moment? I realize I let you and your brother run wild, and now I'm paying the price for it. I'd hoped your role in Albion's death would cause you to wake up—"

Adale slammed her hands down on the table, knocking over all the teacups. Esofi completely failed to bite back a scream at the suddenness of it. Servants were beside her immediately with a hand fan and towels.

"My role?" Adale cried. "Are you *blaming* me?"

"That is not what I said," replied Queen Saski.

"But it's what you meant, isn't it?"

Nobody said anything for a long moment.

Queen Saski gritted her teeth together. "Adale," she said in a very strained voice, "you've gone and spilled the tea."

"I don't care about your tea, I—" Adale glanced over at Esofi, who was still being desperately fanned by a servant, and seemed to come to her senses. Without another word, she began quietly righting the dishes she had knocked over.

"There is to be a hunt tomorrow on the castle hunting grounds," said Adale at last. "You are welcome to join us, Princess."

"Tomorrow?" Esofi hesitated as she thought of all that still needed to be done, weighing it against the prospect of making a good impression on Adale. "I apologize, but I cannot. I've still not visited the temple, and—"

"Don't worry," said Adale. "I know you just got here. Maybe next time."

"Yes," said Esofi. "Certainly the next time."

Queen Saski made a soft noise of exasperation. "All the hunts you children go on, it's a wonder there's a single stag left in those woods. We'll be shipping them in from the countryside soon enough."

"Perhaps we can bring in a boar, then," suggested Adale.

"By Iolar." Queen Saski pressed one hand over her heart.

"Have you ever hunted boar?" Adale asked Esofi.

Esofi shook her head. She had been on many hunts, of course, but had left the baser aspects of it to those who were inclined.

"It is too bad that the dragons have made it so difficult to travel," said Adale wistfully. "Theodoar and I were hoping to visit Vesolda—it's said they hunt bear. Can you imagine?"

"I wouldn't like to," said Queen Saski.

"Oh, I'm sure it's not so bad as that," reassured Adale. "They wouldn't do it if the danger were too great."

Esofi breathed a small laugh. "You are as Albion described."

"What?" Adale looked puzzled.

"Prince Albion often spoke of you in his letters," Esofi explained. "We corresponded frequently for many years."

"I had no idea." Adale seemed stunned. "He wrote of me? What did he say?"

"I do not wish to do his words injustice," murmured Esofi, "but perhaps we shall peruse them together someday. I have all but a few saved. I regret that I lost the early ones. I was young and careless."

"I would like that." Adale's face went so oddly soft that she almost looked like a different person entirely. "Thank you."

Esofi nodded and looked at her gloves.

"How are you liking Ieflaria so far?" asked Adale, who suddenly appeared to have a legitimate interest in her. "You came northward from Gennelet, didn't you? You got to see some of our best farmland."

"It's all so large compared to Rhodia," said Esofi. "And flat too—almost like the sea at rest. It feels strange to look to the distance and see no mountains."

"Did you frequently go to the mountains?" asked Adale.

"If we tried to avoid them, the entire population would be confined to a rather small space," explained Esofi. "Even Rho Dianae is built onto a mountainside. I shall miss being so near to the moon and stars." She already missed the beautiful white marble palace that had been her home, even though she had spent her entire life preparing to leave it behind.

"I can't imagine that's very much fun to farm," observed Adale.

"You must forgive my daughter," Queen Saski interrupted. "She's apparently learned nothing from her tutors."

"It's quite all right," Esofi reassured them both. Then for Adale's benefit, she added, "Rhodia does very little planting—our soil is weak, and only the hardiest of plants will grow in it. We do have our herdsmen and our hunters and our fishermen, but most of our crops are imported from Xytae."

"Ah, to have an ocean between ourselves and Emperor Ionnes," murmured Queen Saski. Though the Xytan Empire was no longer the unstoppable force that it had been so many centuries ago, it still maintained a formidable army. They had never made any indication that they planned to march upon Ieflaria, and they were currently occupied with a campaign in Masim, but Esofi knew that could change at a moment's notice.

"Our primary exports come from our mines and quarries," Esofi explained to Adale. "Emperor Ionnes does so love our white marble, and we are fond of his granaries. Still, I am glad for the distance between our lands."

The sandwiches were ruined, so the meeting came to a premature end. And perhaps it was Esofi's imagination, but Adale seemed not quite so unhappy as she'd been before as they said their farewells.

As Esofi was leaving the gardens, Lisette came to meet her. She had a large, unnervingly artificial smile upon her face.

"There is a man watching you," she managed to say through her smile. "He has been standing behind the rose bushes the entire time."

"How lovely that sounds," Esofi responded warmly.

"He is Theodoar of Leikr, the son of the Marquis of Leikr." Lisette's voice was nearly inaudible, but the long journey together had taught Esofi how to listen for it. "The crown princess entered the garden with him, and he waits for her now."

"It is to be expected," Esofi said loudly, waving her hand as though they were discussing nothing more important than dresses. "Overall, I am not displeased."

Lisette said no more, and so Esofi started off in the direction of her room. Lexandrie was nowhere to be found, but Mireille was waiting in the sitting room and leapt to her feet eagerly when Esofi entered.

"This came for you, Princess!" said Mireille, holding out a stack of parchment. Esofi went to accept it, but Lisette intercepted her, snatching the pages from Mireille's hands and examining each one individually for poisons or powders before passing them on to Esofi.

Esofi scanned the text. It was a marriage contract, nearly identical to the one her parents had signed for her when she was three years old. The only difference seemed to be the name of her groom, but Esofi knew she had to read it carefully to be certain.

"His Majesty's squire came and delivered it while you were gone," explained Mireille. "If you are amenable to the terms, there will be an official signing in two days' time."

"I see," said Esofi. "And where is Lexandrie?"

"She went to speak with Mistress Abbing, that housekeeper," said Mireille. "She dislikes the layout of our room. I think she's going to make those poor servants move our furniture around!"

Esofi gave a little sigh. "Very well. Mireille, will you please send a servant to tell Captain Henris that I require a chest with five thousand pieces of Rhodian gold to be fitted to my carriage and a formal escort to the Great Temple of Iolar? I believe the offering should be made today. If you should happen upon Lexandrie along the way, tell her that I would appreciate her company."

Mireille was off in a flash, and Esofi went into her room to check that she had not become too disheveled during her meeting with the crown princess. She applied a new coat of paint to her lips and then sat down to review the contract His Majesty had sent.

Mireille was the first to return, and Lexandrie shortly thereafter. While Mireille was capable of restraining herself for fear of asking impertinent questions, Lexandrie had no such qualms.

"You met the crown princess, didn't you?" asked Lexandrie, pushing the papers down out of Esofi's face. "What was she like?"

"Tall," said Esofi, turning her body away from her cousin so that she couldn't damage the parchment. "Loud."

"That's what I've heard. They say she's an inebriate." Lexandrie looked pleased with herself for sharing this gossip. "And she has openly declared she does not wish to rule Ieflaria."

"Then it is fortunate that the gods seldom grant wishes," said Esofi, not taking her gaze off the contract.

"Esofi, I'm serious!" huffed Lexandrie. "What if she refuses to take the throne after her parents die? Where will that leave you?"

"There is time enough for that," said Esofi. "Their Majesties are in excellent health. I understand your concerns, Lexandrie, but right now, there is little I can do about Adale's poor ambitions."

Eventually, a servant arrived with the news that Esofi's carriage was ready, and so they all went down to the stables. A combination of royal Ieflarian guards and Rhodian battlemages stood in formation around the carriage, and Captain Henris was talking to another uniformed man. His breastplate was inscribed with the image of a dagger, marking him as a soldier of Reygmadra and the crown.

"Princess," said Captain Henris, turning toward her. "Are you ready?"

"I am," said Esofi. She glanced over at the other man. "Sir."

"This is Captain Lehmann of the royal guard," said Henris. "He has insisted upon adding his own guards to the procession."

Esofi didn't particularly care which soldiers accompanied her to the temple. It was less than two streets away, and she sincerely doubted anyone would be foolish enough to attack a royal carriage in broad daylight on a public street in the most expensive district of Birsgen. But it seemed Captain Henris was interpreting the offer to mean that Lehmann felt the battlemages would not be adequate protection.

Esofi decided not to press the issue. Henris's pride would mend, and she wanted to get to the temple before it filled for evening prayer. She climbed into the carriage, ladies behind her. Resting on the floor was a small wooden chest that held the offering for Iolar.

The gold, jewels, and assorted luxury items that Esofi had brought from Rhodia had been stored in the Birsgenan vaults immediately after their arrival. These vaults were located deep beneath the castle, and everything Esofi had brought would remain there until it was needed, safe and secure, though some would be withdrawn and given to the Temple of Pemele on the day of Esofi's wedding.

The carriage ride was barely fifteen minutes long, and Mireille spent the entire time peeking out the curtains to see how many Birsgeners were gawking.

"Someone needs to sew a dress onto that statue," grumbled Lexandrie. Esofi followed her gaze to the Temple of Dayluue and immediately understood what her cousin meant. Dayluue was the Goddess of Romantic Love, and her iconography reflected that. Dayluue had not been highly regarded back in Rhodia, despite her status as Seventh of the Ten, and sometimes, it seemed like the Rhodian nobility wanted to forget she even existed. But in Ieflaria, the Temple of Dayluue was far more popular. The priestesses even conducted weddings for those who did not feel comfortable in the Temple of Pemele.

When the carriage came to a halt, Esofi waited for a footman to open the door before climbing out onto the front steps of the temple.

The Great Temple of Iolar was the largest religious building in all Ieflaria, but Esofi had only caught a glimpse of it when they'd initially come into the city. Now, with the walkways far less busy, Esofi could appreciate its beauty.

Unlike the majority of the city, which had been built in gray stone and dark wood, the temple was made of gleaming white marble. The sight of it made Esofi momentarily long for the palace that she had grown up in. The outer walls were covered in multiple raised carvings of the sun, the symbol of Iolar, gilded in gold. Two guards had been posted at each golden sun.

Henris came to stand beside Esofi while she waited for the servants to withdraw the offering chest from the carriage. When two of the footmen had it balanced between themselves, she unfurled her parasol and led the procession up the smooth steps into the temple's main courtyard. The temple guards bowed as she passed.

Inside the courtyard was a well-maintained grassy lawn, with a curving path of marble cutting through it. The inner walls were even more ornate than the outer, depicting scenes of caravans traveling on roads, farmers working at their fields, and judges presiding over their courtrooms.

The large doors at the end of the path that led into the interior of the temple opened, and a graying man wearing the garments of an archpriest stepped out. He walked with great purpose, shoulders back and chin held high as his yellow robe fluttered behind him. Sunlight caught the rings on his fingers, casting orbs of multicolored light against the walls. He was not without his own attendants, either. Behind him was an entourage of priests and temple acolytes.

"I have come to pay tribute to Iolar in gratitude for my safe journey from Rhodia," announced Esofi, inching aside so that the footmen could come forward with the chest, which the acolytes were happy to take off their hands. "You will find exactly five thousand gold Rhodian pieces within. Captain?"

Captain Henris withdrew a key from the pocket of his long coat and passed it over to the archpriest.

"Iolar's eyes are upon you, Princess," said the archpriest. "Your devotion has not gone unnoticed."

"I would also like to spend a few moments in the temple in prayer," said Esofi. From behind her, she heard Lexandrie give a quiet groan.

Esofi elected to ignore it.

Chapter Two

ADALE

Despite the rapid downturn that her future appeared to be taking, Crown Princess Adale was anticipating a very good day. She and her waiting ladies, Lethea and Daphene, awoke early that morning, dressed quickly, and headed for the kennels in preparation for the day's hunt.

Unfortunately, their journey was intercepted by two of Adale's father's guards, who informed her that she had a meeting with His Majesty. Over the eighteen years of her life, Adale had bribed countless squires, serving maids, and manservants to claim that they had been unable to find her when her parents summoned. But the guards, soldiers from the temple of Reygmadra, were not so affable. Adale was forced to promise Lethea and Daphene that she would catch up to them later.

Her parents' rooms were behind a massive set of heavy doors carved with symbols of Iolar and gilded in gold. As the guards pulled the doors open for her, Adale was struck by the usual wave of noise. The parlor was filled with various members of the nobility and their servants, all waiting for her parents to emerge from their rooms so the day could officially begin.

Adale missed the days when the nobles were a rainbow of colors, each trying to outshine one another with their attire. But for the past three months, they had only dressed in shades of silver, and the only gemstones worn were pearls or jet.

Adale slipped past them without making eye contact, for she knew a conversation with any senior member of her parents' court would only end in someone trying to make her feel guilty about her assorted failings. She went into her parents' private rooms and shut the doors behind herself to seal off the noise.

Her mother and father were waiting for her, sitting side by side at a table with a stack of papers between them. She stood frozen in the doorway, a little unnerved, and tried to brace herself for whatever lecture was in store.

"Adalheidis," said her father. He was the only one who called her by her birth name. "Come, sit. We need to discuss your future."

Adale went over to the table and sat in the lone remaining chair, moving slowly in an admittedly pathetic attempt to delay the conversation.

"Princess Esofi has agreed to marry you, even after your behavior yesterday," said Saski. "But there is much you must learn if you are to be the queen of Ieflaria. There is so much lost time that we must make up for."

Adale knew what her mother meant. As a child, she had driven her tutors to despair even as Albion excelled at every task they set before him. The young princess's focus was poor, her self-control nonexistent, her energy boundless. Even when she tried to behave more like Albion for her parents' sake, it was always a miserable and short-lived enterprise. By the time she came of age, it seemed her parents had given up on her entirely. All their attention was on Albion, their heir and their hope.

"I can't do it," said Adale.

"It is not a question of whether you can or cannot," said Dietrich. "You *must*. You are the heir to the throne now. Tens of thousands of lives will be on your shoulders. Every single person within our borders will look to you to keep them safe from dragons, pirates, and the Xytan legion."

"Very well, you've convinced me," said Adale, hysterical laughter covering her terror. "I have always wanted to move to Ko'li, and now I finally have a reason! I will pack my things tonight."

"Adale, this is serious!" cried Saski. "You are not so old that you cannot learn to rule, and your father and I do not intend to retire for many years yet. We would not have made you our heir if we believed you were incapable of rising to your station."

"You're wrong!" Adale pleaded. "Pick someone else. Pick anyone else. The twins—"

"Adale, this is how wars start!" shouted Dietrich, rising to his feet so quickly that his chair fell back against the floor. "We have a contract with Rhodia! It is your responsibility to honor it in your brother's place!"

"The twins can honor it!" Adale implored. "They are of the Verheicht family as much as I am. And they can behave—"

"Adale, you are a woman of eighteen, not a child who has yet to master self-control," said Saski, lowering her voice as though she sought to compensate for Dietrich's yelling. "There is nothing Brandt and Svana can do that you are not equally capable of."

That was not even close to the truth, but Adale knew that arguing would only prompt more shouting. Dietrich righted his chair and spoke again.

"You have lived in this castle your entire life," said Dietrich. "You have never been hungry. You have never been cold. When you were ill, healers were sent directly to your bedside. You have never lifted a smith's hammer, never milked a goat, never tilled a field. You have never labored until your hands bled. You have never known the fear that your home might be nothing but cinders in a week's time. It has been pleasant, hasn't it?"

"Yes, but..." began Adale.

"Did you think you owed Ieflaria nothing in return for your idyllic, prolonged childhood?"

"That's not fair," protested Adale. "I never asked for it. I never asked for any of it!"

"The girl who scrubs your floors did not ask for her life, either," said Dietrich.

"The girl who scrubs my floors cannot be forced to marry a stranger!"

"And that is my point entirely," said Dietrich. "The lives of our ordinary citizens are not nearly as comfortable as ours. But in return, their responsibilities are not so heavy. Small mistakes are easily forgiven. Even large mistakes seldom result in the deaths of thousands. And when they return to their homes after a day's work, they are freed from their responsibilities until the sun rises once more. I am the king of Ieflaria every moment of my life, waking and sleeping. No decision that I make is insignificant. The smallest lapse in judgment could cause untold damage to our nation, and even to our continent. Our people understand this, and that is why they allow us to live as we do. It is not entitlement, Adale. It is an exchange. You have enjoyed all the benefits of our station and none of the burdens. You are correct when you say it is unfair, but you fail to realize that it has been unfair entirely in your favor."

Saski pushed the papers aside and looked at her daughter. "Our subjects trust us, Adale. We are able to live like this because they believe we will sacrifice anything for their well-being, even our own freedom. And they trust us to treat them fairly, as equals. Your cousins may know how to appear honorable to their fellow nobles, but you know they have nothing but contempt for the common citizens of Ieflaria. Do you think they could rule with compassion?"

Adale could not hide her shock. She had never heard anyone speak of her cousins in such a way. She had never heard anyone imply they were imperfect.

"You did not think we had noticed?" asked Saski, accurately interpreting the expression on Adale's face. "The twins are not as sly as they believe themselves to be. Know this: your cousins will only be permitted to marry Princess Esofi as a last resort. We have spent decades cultivating the goodwill of our people. We are reluctant to allow those two to throw it away."

Adale could hardly speak. She felt as though she had just been run over by a carriage. There was a very good chance she would be sick if she did not escape the room immediately. She turned her thoughts to the poor maid who would be assigned to clean it up in order to keep her stomach under control. "I-I need to think. I didn't know. I...I need to think."

"I think that would be wise," agreed her mother.

Adale fled.

ADALE'S HORSE WAS a tall, dark bay stallion named Warcry. He was a stubborn creature, but he loved the hunts as much as his rider. By the time she arrived at the stables, he was already saddled and ready to go.

Daphene and Lethea spent the entire ride to the royal hunting grounds trying to wheedle a few words from her, asking her what her parents wanted and what the status of her engagement was. But Adale merely pressed her lips together and refused to look any of them in the face until they grew bored and gave up.

The party met at the usual place just within the borders of the hunting grounds. The royal huntsman and his dogs were waiting to direct the nobles to their quarry, a stag that he had been tracking for the past few days. But Adale found that she could not focus on his words today. All that her parents had said to her was running through her mind.

The Ieflarian nobility was relatively new, for Ieflaria had been a territory of the Xytan Empire until a mere three hundred years ago, when the empire's power had waned enough for its outermost territories to declare their independence. Adale's ancestors had been the first regents of Ieflaria, and had sworn they would rule very differently from the Xytan emperors.

The result was the very philosophy that her parents had shared with her that morning. Adale had heard endless variations on it throughout her childhood, but it had always seemed so abstract, until today.

Theodoar seemed to notice her distraction and pulled his horse up alongside her to prod her boot with his own, which of course began a subtle kicking fight, but Adale was smiling by the end of it.

The hunt began, and for a while, all was leisurely and pleasant. Theodoar rode by her side, speaking of all the things Adale needed to hear—namely, everything that wasn't a wedding or a princess.

But soon enough, the forest warmed under the slowly rising sun and the gossip began in earnest.

"Crown Princess!" sang out Lady Brigit, and Adale flinched at the sound of her new title. "Is it true that your fiancée gave ten thousand gold pieces to the temple yesterday?"

"I've no fiancée yet," retorted Adale. Her chest suddenly felt odd, constricted. She was having difficulty breathing. "And what she does with her money is her own concern."

"It was not ten thousand when you told it this morning, Brigit," called Lord Baldric from somewhere in the rear.

"I forgot!" huffed Lady Brigit. "That's why I was asking!"

"I've only spoken to her once," said Adale, keeping her gaze locked upon the forest path ahead. Her breath was short and shallow, her palms drenching the leather reins in sweat. "She told me nothing of her plans to pay tribute."

"Then what did you speak of?" Brigit called, prompting much laughter from the party. "Come, Adale, you have told us nothing! Do you wish us to go mad from wondering?"

Up until that moment, Adale had always enjoyed the openness and informality of the nobles she'd chosen to associate herself with, and the fact that such behavior would scandalize her parents had only been part of the appeal. Her social group was made up almost entirely of second-, third-, or even fourth-born children of the Ieflarian nobility. With no titles to inherit unless four or five people died in rapid succession and no significant obligations upon any given day of the year, they spent their time roaming from city to city, enjoying their parents' wealth and accomplishing nothing of note. It was a life Adale had always loved, and the fact that she commanded little respect had never bothered her until this moment.

"I say nothing because there is nothing to say," said Adale at last. "She is still a stranger to me." Perhaps she always would be. Perhaps it would be easier that way.

"Did you not invite her today?" asked Gauslen. Gauslen was a neutroi and used the title "Noble" rather than Lord or Lady.

"I did," said Adale. "But she has only just arrived, and declined the invitation."

"That's a pity," sighed Brigit from somewhere nearby. "I think her figure would benefit from a day upon horseback."

It was a relief to finally have something to yell about.

"Brigit!" snapped Adale. "I'll tolerate your stupid questions because I know you lack the wit to keep them to yourself, but you have no right to insult Esofi! She has done more for the benefit of Ieflaria in these past three days than you have in your entire life!"

"I am only speaking the truth!" retorted Brigit. "Does she not remind you of a tiered cake?" There was some tittering from the back at these words. "Besides, even if she was Dayluue given mortal form, her temperament is not at all suited for yours. She will drive you mad! Perhaps you ought to leave her to one of your cousins."

"And then abdicate entirely and live out my life with you ruffians?" asked Adale darkly. She had occasionally joked darkly about the possibility, before she had known her parents had objections to her cousins. Now it seemed she was even more trapped than ever before.

"Only if my princess wished it," Brigit said with a dramatic toss of her braids. "And you do wish it, do you not?"

Adale looked at Theodoar for help. Besides Albion, there was no one who had ever known her mind as well as him. But he only shrugged.

"It would certainly be more satisfying than ruling Ieflaria," he said. But before Adale could respond, the horns sounded and the chase began. In that moment, Adale forgot everything, save for the thrill of the gallop and the crying of the hounds.

Soon enough, the hunters had the stag at bay. The hounds were restrained to keep them from stealing the day's kill, and Adale dismounted and drew her sword. As the highest-ranking member of the party, it was her right to make the kill or grant it to another. Today, there was nobody in the party that she didn't feel like kicking in the head, and so she chose to keep it for herself.

Once the stag was dead, the huntsman came forward to help her finish cutting the carcass into pieces. The meat would be delivered to the kitchens, and the rest would be made into trophies. Adale fed a few small pieces of meat to the dogs as a reward for their help.

Adale remounted and let her thoughts wander as the others gossiped and shouted to one another. She wasn't looking forward to returning home tonight and wished that she could make a rapid excursion to the countryside without her parents ordering her home to court Esofi properly.

It wasn't that Adale disliked Esofi; she didn't know her well enough for that. From the little she had seen, Esofi struck her as very formal but also very gentle. Yes, she was not as thin or as tall as the average Ieflarian, but Adale did not think that was a bad thing. She looked *warm*, Adale decided, for lack of a better descriptor. Warm and soft.

But Esofi seemed to represent everything Adale had never wanted. Her only consolation was that Esofi probably didn't want her, either.

Maybe the princess could be convinced to marry one of her cousins. Her parents wouldn't like it, but they just weren't being reasonable. Yes, the twins could not be accused of being *kind*, but surely that was secondary to competence? Her parents claimed Adale was capable of rising to her station, but parents always overestimated the qualities of their children, didn't they? Adale felt a twinge of confidence return. She knew herself better than anyone else. She knew her cousins would be better regents, if only by default.

Adale rode slowly on the way back to the castle, with only Theodoar beside her. At some point, someone broke out the flasks, but Adale found that she wasn't inclined to drink that night. Her friends went on ahead, laughing and screeching into the dusk.

"What do you think?" asked Adale quietly.

"I think you're already miserable," said Theodoar. "Imagine how much worse it will be once you are married."

"That is not helpful, Theodoar!" Adale snapped.

"It is the truth," said Theodoar. "I see your unhappiness. Everyone does. But you don't have to marry her. Your parents wouldn't be pleased, but they would not disown you. Let her have one of your cousins, and live your life the way you have always meant to."

"Perhaps," said Adale. But something still seemed to be holding her back. Was it her parents' words or her memory of Albion? She had no idea how her brother had managed to live his life in the way he had, a perfect balance between obligation and revelry, never too rigid or too irresponsible. And he'd always been able to speak with their parents openly without angering them, an art Adale had never mastered.

He would have been...he would have been a good husband for Esofi, a good king for Ieflaria.

"You are still uncertain," said Theodoar. "Why? What is there to debate?"

"I don't know," admitted Adale. "I can't explain it. And becoming queen is only half of the problem. I'd have to marry a foreigner I barely know. And I know it's foolish and selfish for a princess to expect she'll be allowed to marry whoever she likes, but my parents always promised they'd let me pick for myself because—"

Because Albion was there to be the responsible one.

And now he was gone.

"At least speak to her," Theodoar urged. "See if she would be open to breaking off the betrothal in favor of one of your cousins. And then we can leave for my parents' estate before Their Majesties find out. We can hide out in the lodge if they send guards. And by the time we return, they'll have forgotten their anger, and things will go back to the way they ought to be."

"Perhaps," said Adale, guilt filling her heart as she thought of her parents' true opinion of the twins. Still, Theodoar sounded completely certain, and it was difficult not to smile when he seemed so optimistic. "I suppose it's just...she seems so delicate. I do not wish to hurt her."

"It's not personal, Adale. It's politics," Theodoar reminded her.

"And if she refuses?" questioned Adale. "Do we just run anyway and hope for the best?"

"Perhaps," said Theodoar, but now his eyes were distant with thought.

They rode back to the stables in silence. When they arrived, the young nobles were already making plans to go into the city and patronize a string of taverns. It was nothing too unusual, especially after a day like the one they'd had. But Adale found herself wanting nothing more than to fall into bed and forget the world for a few hours, and so she bid them all good night and began the journey back to her rooms.

As Adale dragged her feet across the carpets, she heard a burst of conversation in a language she didn't understand, followed by some sweet, gentle laughter. She looked up and saw Esofi and all three of her waiting ladies walking toward her, moving slowly in their heavy Rhodian dresses. Esofi was dressed in a pale-blue gown with lacy white ruffles and white silk flowers sewn onto every available surface. There was even a tiny matching bonnet perched on the top of her curls.

Adale had never had a care for her appearance in her life, but now she felt oddly self-conscious in her riding clothes. She had no mirror, but she could only imagine how she must look to the ladies of Rhodia. Adale risked a glance down at herself, and saw with great relief that there did not appear to be any bloodstains on her coat or trousers.

"My lady!" Esofi had noticed her at last. "Have you just returned from your hunt?"

"I... Yes, Princess," said Adale. Esofi came to a halt, leaving a few prudent steps between them. Esofi's ladies were whispering to each other behind their fans, but the princess did not seem to notice. The smile on her round, earnest face seemed genuine, though Adale knew that it wasn't a guarantee of anything.

"I hope nobody was injured?" pressed Esofi.

Adale shook her head. "No, everything was as planned." She paused awkwardly, unsure of how to continue. Surely Esofi did not want to hear the details of how she'd killed the stag.

"I've been trying to learn the layout of the castle," explained Esofi. "I do hate to trouble the servants for directions when they're so busy. But I shall have it soon enough, I think."

"Oh," said Adale. "Well, uh..."

"I also met with Their Majesties today," continued Esofi. "I've reviewed the marriage contract and found it to my liking. I suppose I will see you tomorrow, then?"

"Tomorrow?" repeated Adale, wondering if she was being dismissed.

"At the ceremonial signing," prompted Esofi. When Adale said nothing, Esofi added, "Of the marriage contract."

"Tomorrow?" Adale just barely kept a shriek out of her voice. "It's so soon?"

"Surely my lady was informed," said Esofi, worry entering her soft brown eyes for a moment. And now that she mentioned it, Adale did seem to recall her father's squire, Ilbert, telling her something about something happening on some date, and her presence would be required, but...

"Oh." Adale's voice sounded as though she'd just been punched in the gut. "Naturally."

Esofi did not look to be particularly reassured, and Adale supposed she could not blame her.

"I have also added some conditions of my own to the contract," explained Esofi. Adale froze as her mind was flooded with one horrible scenario after the other. Had the princess added a personal code of conduct for Adale? A ban on drinking? Or hunting? Or riding? Or anything that wasn't sitting quietly in prayer? "Their Majesties were quite happy with the additions."

That cemented it for Adale. It was a ban on drinking!

"Oh." Adale tried to remember if she had enough linens in her bedchamber to construct a rope long enough to climb out the window and flee Ieflaria forever. "Well, I...I should want to review that, then, I suppose..."

"I would like it if you did." Esofi's eyes were warm again. "We've had none of your input so far. I feel as though I'm marrying your parents, not you."

Now was the time to mention her cousins, Adale realized with a small sinking feeling in her heart. She hadn't wanted it to be like this, an abrupt declaration in a hallway, but things were moving so quickly. It might even be the only chance she ever got. If only there were more time!

How to phrase it, though? Adale was so clumsy with words. Surely, she'd find the worst possible way to convey the sentiment. And then Esofi would be so disappointed and hurt, and she might even cry, and then Esofi's smallest lady, the one who looked like a snake transfigured into a girl, would step forward with venom spitting from her teeth and—

"Well," said Esofi brightly. "We mustn't be late for the sundown service. Good night to you, Crown Princess Adale."

"I...but...yes." *Coward!* Adale cursed herself. *You worthless, worthless coward.* "Good night, Princess Esofi."

The ladies departed, leaving Adale standing there alone but for her racing heart.

Adale all but ran back to her rooms, hands trembling. It took a moment to open her door because the key kept missing the lock. Once inside, she hurried to her writing desk, which was seldom used, and searched the drawer for ink and paper. She took a few long breaths to settle herself and then composed a quick note.

> *Theodoar—*
>
> *I have failed utterly. The signing of the marriage contract is to be tomorrow. I will not have enough time to propose our solution to the princess. Shall we go tonight? Respond quickly.*
>
> *A*

Adale folded and sealed the note with wax, blowing impatiently on it to make it cool faster. Once it was dry, or dry enough, Adale went out into the hallway and grabbed a passing page boy by the shoulder.

"Deliver this to Lord Theodoar immediately," she ordered, shoving the note into his hand. "Return with a response tonight and there will be three gold coins in it for you."

The page, who had probably been headed to the nightly service at the orders of whomever was in charge of him, brightened up and bolted off like a rabbit. Adale felt confident that even if Theodoar was not inclined to reply out of disgust for her failure, the page would badger him until he'd sent something in response.

Adale changed into her nightclothes simply to pass the time and paced around her quarters, occasionally stopping to rearrange some trophies. For some reason, her breathing was only coming in sharp, shallow bursts and her hands would not stop shaking. She was going to start kicking furniture over if she did not have a response soon.

The ringing of the bells signaled the start of the sundown service, but Adale ignored them. She'd always thought of the evening services as an even greater waste of time than the morning ones.

Since Albion's death, Adale had barely set foot in the castle chapel or any of the great temples in Birsgen, except on certain holy days where the fight with her mother was more trouble than simply attending. She did not care. Everyone knew that the temples were corrupt, collecting mountains of tribute and speaking their own words in the place of long-absent gods.

At long, long last, the page boy returned. Adale gave him five coins instead of the promised three and tore the note open.

> *Adale*
>
> *Fear not, I have a plan to buy us more time. Tomorrow, act as usual and speak as usual. I will take care of the rest. Trust me.*
>
> *Theodoar*

Adale read the note over a few times in shock. Theodoar did not wish to leave immediately? He had a plan? The idea of Theodoar with a plan left her feeling uneasy, and she hoped Esofi was not in any danger.

Adale turned the note over, scrawled the words *What are you going to do?* on the back, and gave it to the page boy. And though she waited all through the night, waking at every hour with her heart threatening to dance out of her chest, a reply never came.

AT THE RINGING of the morning bell, Adale tumbled out of bed and hit the floor with a soft thump. She stayed there for a moment, contemplating the possibility of throwing herself from the window and putting her suffering to an end. Fortunately, or unfortunately, Lady Lethea was somehow alert enough after last night's revelries to hear that her lady was awake and stumbled in to help her.

Adale usually disdained having help when she was dressing, but that day, she was glad for the extra set of hands.

"You are not well at all," observed Lady Lethea. "Is it the princess?"

"What else?" asked Adale. "And...I believe Theodoar may be planning something foolish."

"That's unusual only in that you have not been included in the preparations," pointed out Lady Lethea.

"Perhaps," said Adale. "But...I am worried. Though I suppose he would never harm someone."

"Harm someone?" Lethea met Adale's eyes. "How do you mean?"

"I don't know," admitted Adale.

"You truly aren't well," repeated Lethea, pressing her hand to Adale's forehead. "All this worrying! Don't you dare turn into your mother."

That, at least, made Adale laugh. "Very well, you've persuaded me. Let's go to breakfast. They will all be shocked to see us awake at this hour."

So, leaving Daphene to sleep off her headache, they went down to the banquet hall where all meals were served. Adale had a feeling that Esofi would be there and was looking forward to a reassurance that the princess was unharmed and, hopefully, still oblivious to Theodoar's plans.

Adale had never been early for breakfast before, let alone on time, so it was a bit of a novelty that the servants were setting everything out in preparation. Beside her, Lethea yawned.

"Why have I agreed to come here?" she murmured. A servant drew the heavy drapes open with a great flourish, flooding the room with morning light, and Lethea flinched as though he'd brandished a sword at her.

"Over here," said Adale, heading for a seat that would give her a full view of the doors so that she might see Esofi the moment that she entered. Unfortunately, the meal would not begin until the arrival of Adale's parents, and so there was no food to keep her occupied in the meantime.

As the minutes passed, Adale began to worry that Esofi had decided to take breakfast in her own rooms or that something had befallen her. But surely if something had happened to the princess, the servants would be talking about it?

Soon enough, Esofi and her ladies entered. As foreigners, they were the only ones not required to dress in the mourning colors, and their bright dresses stood out against the servants and nobles in their dull shades of black and gray and occasional purples. Adale was glad that the mourning period would soon be over. She felt that she shouldn't have to be reminded of her brother's death every time she looked at someone.

Esofi must have sensed Adale's attention upon her and met her gaze with a bright smile. Her gown that day was a pleasant shade of palest pink with puffed sleeves that ended just below the shoulder to accommodate long gloves made of lace. The fabric of her skirt had been pulled up and twisted into bows around the knee, revealing a second layer of ivory skirts beneath, embroidered and trimmed with pearls. Esofi somehow managed to take her seat without ruining any of it.

But before Adale could speak to her, the doors opened again and Their Majesties entered. Adale reflected that she seldom actually saw her parents unless they needed to shout at her personally rather than via a squire or servant.

"Adale!" said Queen Saski, not bothering to hide the shock in her tone as she spotted her daughter at the table. Immediately, all eyes were upon her. Adale tried not to glower. "You've come to a meal! Or perhaps I have been poisoned and am in the throes of hallucination."

"I've come for the meal, not for you," retorted Adale, but her words were lost in the shuffle of places as everyone in the room moved so that Adale could sit by her parents. Adale protested every step of the way, but it was no use and eventually she found herself in the chair beside her mother.

At least she was a bit nearer to Esofi, not that she could say anything important to her with her parents so close.

Esofi seemed to be eating surprisingly little, and was more concerned with answering her mother's questions than anything else. Adale forced herself to pay attention, but they didn't actually seem to be discussing anything important, merely a tour of the city that Esofi hoped to take soon.

Adale realized that her attention had drifted back to Esofi's face again. There was such a warmth and softness about her that Adale found herself feeling relieved that she hadn't mentioned her cousins last night.

In fact, for some reason, she found that the idea didn't seem quite as satisfying as it had the day before. Adale's parents' assessment of her cousins the previous morning had been frighteningly accurate. If one of the twins was allowed to sit on the throne, the entire castle staff might give notice. And what about Esofi?

Adale glanced over at the princess. It would be like a rabbit marrying a wolf. The palace staff might be able to hold their own for a while and always had the option of leaving to find better employment, but Esofi would be trapped forever. Could Adale really leave someone, even a stranger, to such a fate?

Perhaps...perhaps if Adale did marry Esofi, it wouldn't be as bad as she was anticipating.

Adale gave her head a shake. Was she going *mad*? Even if Esofi made a pleasant bride, there was no way Adale would be anything other than the most shameful queen in Ieflarian history. She forced herself to remember the threats her father had listed: dragons, pirates, the Xytan legion. Adale did not have the fortitude to contend with such issues.

Breakfast came to an end with the departure of the king and queen, who first made Adale swear that she would be at the signing of the contract in front of all the important members of the court that afternoon. When they were finally gone, Adale and Esofi seemed to come to an unspoken agreement and walked from the hall together, their ladies trailing behind.

"Have you plans for the day until the signing?" asked Adale. Perhaps if she stayed by Esofi's side until then, she could make sure Theodoar's plan did not cause the princess any harm.

"Certainly nothing that cannot be postponed," said Esofi, looking up at Adale with hope in her eyes. "Now that we've settled the issue of stationing the battlemages, I've found myself with far fewer worries."

"The battlemages?" repeated Adale. She vaguely remembered hearing something about that.

"To defend against the dragons," said Esofi. "Your country has withstood them admirably, but it's really wiser to engage them with Talcia's magic. There will be far fewer casualties. When I first arrived, many were hoping a battlemage could be assigned to each particular location. Yesterday, I had to convince the Temple of Reygmadra that most battlemages are not powerful enough to defeat a dragon alone. The archpriestess was not pleased, but everyone agreed that we must take time to determine where the mages are needed most."

"Oh," said Adale. The Temple of Reygmadra, Goddess of Warfare and Eighth of the Ten, commanded Ieflaria's military. They were the largest of the Eleven temples in Ieflaria, and second only to the Temple of Iolar in influence. Adale could not help but be impressed by Esofi standing up to the archpriestess. "The dragons have troubled us for as long as anyone can remember, but in recent years, it's become...excessive. Nobody seems to know why."

"Dragons can smell the presence of wealth," Esofi explained. "Precious metals and jewels have a scent to them, like meat or bread. Legends say they were once wise and reasonable creatures and even had the ability to speak. But as mankind grew civilized under Iolar's guidance, we began to draw more wealth from the earth and the temptation became too great to resist any longer. When Talcia realized what they had become, she took their wisdom away and they became like animals. I suspect your nation is only suffering from these attacks because their population has grown too large for their islands. If we can cull their numbers, the worst of the attacks should cease."

Adale realized that Esofi seemed to be walking in the direction of the castle's chapel, but she wasn't sure if this was intentional or not.

"How do you intend to do that?" asked Adale. "You wouldn't send soldiers to the Silver Isles, would you?"

"Oh goodness, no!" said Esofi. "That would be a death sentence. There must be hundreds, perhaps thousands of dragons on those islands. Nobody can fight that many all at once."

"You seem to be quite certain of things," said Adale. She wondered if she would be equally confident if she hadn't been such a terrible student.

"Not all things," replied Esofi. "Only the few which I have been educated for. But few kingdoms can say they boast a mastery of magic in the way Rhodia does, and so I suppose that makes me valuable."

Esofi paused as they reached the doors of the Chapel of the Ten. They were painted with a scene of Iolar and Talcia standing before the sun and the moon, respectively. The two reached for one another, their fingertips meeting briefly where the two doors fit together.

"Did you wish to go in?" asked Adale.

"No, I think not," Esofi mused. "I do love this design, though. I see so little of Talcia in your country. She must be feeling neglected, I think."

"Oh." If there was anything Adale thought of less often than the worship of the gods, she could not recall it.

"Do you know how many babies are born in Ieflaria with Talcia's magic?" asked Esofi. "I asked Archmage Eads yesterday. One in ten thousand."

"That's bad?" guessed Adale.

"I've never heard of worse." Esofi shook her head, setting her curls bouncing. "But this must be why. Once we restore her worship, she will look upon Ieflaria more kindly. I only wonder how she managed to fall out of favor to begin with."

Adale said nothing. She had always been of the opinion that if the gods truly did exist, they cared little for Inthya below. But Esofi spoke of them as though she knew them personally.

"I've been told that your parents will take petitions today," said Esofi. "I would like very much to observe them."

"Oh," said Adale in surprise. "If you'd like." Once every month, her parents would open the castle gates and grant audiences with common Ieflarians. It usually ended in sending out more supplies and soldiers to small settlements that she had never heard of. Adale had not been to one since Albion's death, for he was no longer there to urge her into attendance.

"My parents only opened their throne room once every six months," said Esofi. "I suppose since Rhodia's population is so much lower than Ieflaria's, there was less of a need. I am eager to see what issues your citizens find most pressing."

"It will be nothing but requests for aid against the dragons," predicted Adale. "They're striking all across the country. It's strange—they'll cross our borders and fly peacefully for days, unless intercepted. Then suddenly they'll decide they've had enough of a certain town. You'd expect they'd simply attack the first settlement they come upon."

"Yes, I had heard," Esofi murmured.

"Well, let's hope they don't ruin too much of our harvest this year," said Adale. "I don't know how much we have left in the storehouses."

"You don't?" Esofi gave her that wide-eyed look of surprise that Adale was rapidly growing accustomed to.

"Here, the throne room is this way," said Adale quickly. "If we don't hurry, we'll have to stand in the back."

In fact, they still had about half an hour before the audiences began, but something about the line of conversation was making Adale feel terribly inadequate.

Albion would have known, an ugly voice inside of her chastised. *Albion could have told her exactly how many grains of wheat are left in the storehouses.*

They reached the throne room as it was beginning to fill, and Adale took a spot near to her parents' thrones, determined to show that she could be a responsible heir if she chose to be. Knight Commander Glaed was already there in his usual place, with Sir Livius just behind him. Both wore chain mail beneath dazzlingly white tabards, marked on the chest with an image of the sun.

Adale supposed they'd been there for an hour, probably discussing the evils of sleeping in late and eating cake. She could not understand why a person might be compelled to join the Order of the Sun.

"Crown Princess," the Knight Commander said, not completely managing to keep a note of surprise from his voice.

"Don't start with me, Glaed," said Adale darkly. On top of swearing off drinking, gambling, and having any sort of fun at all, Paladins of the Sun were also forbidden to tell even the smallest of lies. Because of that, Glaed had never disguised his disapproval of her. But it seemed Glaed wasn't in the mood to criticize her today, and instead, he turned his gaze to Esofi.

"It is an honor, Princess," he said, bowing deeply. "I am Glaed of Armoth, Knight Commander of the Order of the Sun in Ieflaria. My companion is Sir Livius, formerly Knight Commander of the Order of the Sun in Xytae. We are both at your service."

"Thank you, Knight Commander," said Esofi. "I am told your paladins have been instrumental in protecting Ieflaria's people. It is fortunate that you are so numerous here—I don't think I've gone more than a day without seeing a paladin somewhere since I stepped off the ship."

"The Order of the Sun has withdrawn their support from the Xytan Empire," said Sir Livius. He was a Xytan native, tall and olive-skinned with silver streaking his dark hair. "For many years, Emperor Ionnes overstepped himself and paid tribute to Reygmadra above Iolar. Still, for the sake of defending the people of Xytae, we intended to remain loyal. But last autumn, the emperor announced that we would join his soldiers in Masim."

Adale remembered the outrage that had followed the announcement. The Order of the Sun did not wage wars of conquest, and she couldn't imagine what Emperor Ionnes must have been thinking to even attempt to order such a thing. The Paladins of the Sun stationed in his empire might have been his citizens, but everyone knew they were more akin to priests than soldiers.

"I sent a courier to the Justices," continued Sir Livius, naming the highest tier of the Order of the Sun. "They ordered all those who were stationed within Xytae's borders to find more worthy posts. Some went to Masim to aid the Masimi in defending their homeland from Xytae. But most of us could not bear the thought of fighting our own countrymen and came to Ieflaria instead."

"It is fortunate that you did not have to go so far from your home," said Esofi. "I hope that someday Emperor Ionnes will be penitent and allow you to return."

Not too soon, though, thought Adale. *We need their protection far more than Xytae does.*

"I do as well," Sir Livius said, inclining his head. "Every sunrise, I pray that he comes to see reason. But I fear I will not see my homeland again until the day he joins Asterium."

Adale was surprised at the admission, since she had never heard any of the paladins speak of longing for anything. But Esofi only nodded in silent understanding.

"Oh look," said Adale as a familiar yellow-clad figure entered the room. "Knight Commander, it's your dearest companion."

It was very amusing to see Glaed's jaw clench at the sight of the archpriest. One might be inclined to believe the two would find common ground in their shared devotion to Iolar, but this was not the case. It seemed that the only thing the two agreed upon was their mutual disdain.

"Pompous, prideful, corrupt old man," Glaed muttered. "What does he believe he can do for the petitioners? Squeeze a few more coins from them?"

"Watch this, I'm going to see if I can get them to fight," Adale told Esofi.

"Adale!" scolded Esofi.

But any minor scandal that Adale might have orchestrated was averted by the arrival of King Dietrich and Queen Saski. The co-regents took their seats, and the first petitioner of the day was shown in.

As Adale had predicted, it was a man from a northern town, asking for more guards and more supplies. He was a woodsman by trade and expressed fear that the dragons would burn down the forests if there weren't more soldiers stationed in the north.

"Archpriestess Gerta has repeatedly stated that there are no more soldiers in the Ieflarian army left to send without removing protection from another settlement," King Dietrich said. He looked to Knight Commander Glaed. "Can any paladins be reassigned?"

"Our priority is the farmlands in the south," said Glaed. "If the dragons burn our fields before the harvest, it will not matter how many soldiers are stationed at our borders."

"But the dragons are attacking from the north!" cried the woodsman. "Our lands are nearest to the Silver Isles. We are in far greater danger! We are citizens of Ieflaria as much as any farmer. Are we not entitled to the same protections?"

Now Adale remembered why she never attended these audiences. They made her want to crawl into her bed and never return to the awful outside world.

"Woodsman," said King Dietrich, "I would grant you your request if I had even a single soldier to spare. But I do not. Nor does the Order of the Sun. I will grant you all the supplies your people need, but—"

"What about her?" demanded the man, turning to point directly at Esofi, drawing shocked gasps and murmurs from the crowd. "The entire country saw her arrive with her army! Or are they meant to huddle around the castle and protect the royalty alone?"

"Woodsman," repeated King Dietrich in a far less gracious tone than the one he'd been using a moment before. "You forget yourself."

"Am I wrong to expect protection from my future queen?" Desperation, it seemed, had overcome the man's common sense. "Why is she here, if not to save us from the dragons?"

The guards were already coming forward, and Adale felt pity for the man. But Esofi raised her hand, and they paused.

"May I speak?" she asked.

There was no movement in the throne room for a long moment. After sharing a glance with Queen Saski, King Dietrich nodded.

Adale could see the tremble of Esofi's jaw, but when she spoke, her voice betrayed no anxiety.

"Woodsman," Esofi said. "I understand your fear and your frustration. There is no rapid solution, which is difficult to hear in such desperate times. Yes, I brought battlemages to Ieflaria with me. But my mages are few in number, and we must assign them judiciously, or else their journey will have been for naught. We have not yet decided where they will be assigned, but I swear to you that I will remember your words when it comes time to send them to their posts. Can you accept this?"

Adale was surprised to notice that Esofi's entire body was now tensed, as though she was expecting the man to leap forward and strike her. But the man seemed to relax. He lowered his head and nodded.

"I think this petition is complete," said King Dietrich. "You may report to the storehouses for aid. One of the clerks will assist you. Who is next?"

Adale turned to Esofi, who was still staring at the space where the woodsman had stood.

"Are you all right?" she asked.

"The princess needs air," said the tallest of Esofi's ladies, gripping Esofi by the arm. Lexandrie? Was that her name? "Come, this room is far too crowded anyway."

Lexandrie steered Esofi from the room, with the other two hurrying after. Meanwhile, the second group of petitioners had come in and were beginning to complain to the king and queen that the priestesses of Dayluue had put *that* statue out again.

Adale looked at Lethea. "Come on, we have to go after them."

"Do we?" asked Lethea. "I want to hear this."

Adale grabbed her friend and dragged her after the Ieflarians. They passed more petitioners waiting outside but did not stop until they'd reached a quieter area of the palace. Adale was able to direct them to a sitting room, which fortunately was not in use when they arrived. Esofi sank down onto one of the sofas, while the youngest waiting lady fanned her with a handkerchief.

"The nerve of him!" seethed the girl. "Does nobody in this country have any manners?"

"Why did you bother to respond to him?" demanded Lexandrie, as if she thought she were Esofi's mother. "He didn't deserve your words."

"He was frightened," Esofi protested. "And the guards were going to throw him out."

"They should have!"

"For not wanting to be eaten by a dragon? Is that a crime?"

Esofi and Lexandrie glared at each other for a long moment.

"Don't fight," said the youngest waiting lady. "It turned out all right, didn't it? He got an answer and he left."

"He was not entitled to any answers, Mireille!" Lexandrie snapped.

Adale suddenly felt an appreciation for her own waiting ladies, whom she had been allowed to select for herself. She couldn't imagine having to endure being assigned whomever her mother picked.

"Enough," said Esofi. "Both of you, please."

In the ensuing silence, Adale slid into the space beside Esofi. "Are you well?"

Esofi gave a brittle laugh. "Oh, of course I am. I was just a little startled. I've never been spoken to in such a way by a commoner. My guard was down. Do you think I responded well?" She looked into Adale's eyes earnestly, and Adale felt her face begin to grow uncomfortably warm.

"I do," said Adale.

Esofi nodded to herself. "At home, I was always comfortable around the lower classes because I knew they would never second-guess me," she said in a low voice. "Even if I said something very silly. But everything is so different here. I feel as though I am off-balance."

"That was unusual, even for our outspoken people," Adale reassured her. "Our citizens might not be so formal as Rhodia's, but they are respectful. I believe he only singled you out because he was desperate."

"You are probably right," Esofi agreed. "Do you truly believe I responded well? Perhaps I should have done a better job of explaining—"

"Now you're being silly!" cried Adale. For a moment, Esofi stared at her with an expression of pure shock, but then she saw the smile on Adale's face and began to smile as well.

"Pardon me, Your Highnesses," said a new voice. Adale looked around to see a servant standing just outside the doorway. He had a sealed letter clutched in one hand. "I've a message for Princess Esofi from Lord Theodoar of Leikr."

Adale's heart sank. She'd almost forgotten about this part.

Esofi looked surprised but accepted the envelope. "Lord Theodoar. He's one of your entourage, isn't he?"

"I..." Adale looked at the note helplessly, wondering if there was any way she could snatch it away without looking like she had been struck mad. Esofi was already breaking the seal and unfolding it.

"How very odd," said Esofi after a long pause. "He says that there is a matter of great importance he wishes to discuss with me." Esofi looked up at Adale. "Do you have any idea what this might be about?"

Adale felt that this was a very unfair question.

"He asks me to meet with him in the east courtyard." Esofi frowned, her white face powder leaving a crease behind in her forehead.

"Allow me to accompany you, then," said Adale. "Theodoar is my trusted friend, and I do not believe he would mean you harm, but I'm afraid he might be about to do something foolish."

Esofi looked up at Adale again, a flicker of suspicion in her face. "Very well. If you will show me the way? I fear I have forgotten."

"Of course," said Adale. But then Esofi got to her feet and strode from the room, hands clutching so tightly at her parasol that Adale thought she might splinter the wooden handle. Adale made the mistake of glancing back at Esofi's ladies. None of them were smiling. The littlest one looked Adale directly in the eyes, her face as cold as marble. Then, very slowly, she raised one finger up to her own pale neck and drew a line across it.

"This is not my fault," Adale muttered through gritted teeth. "This is everyone's fault except mine!"

But it seemed that Esofi had not required directions at all and successfully led them to the courtyard without a word. Theodoar's familiar silhouette was waiting on the green, and he was not alone. His own servants were there, along with some of the nobles who had been on the hunt yesterday.

Esofi did not falter in her step, though the waiting lady who had just threatened to murder Adale pushed ahead so that she and the princess were shoulder to shoulder.

"Princess Esofi of Rhodia," said Theodoar as she approached. "And...Adale?"

"Lord Theodoar," Esofi replied. "I received your message. Is all well?"

Theodoar pulled himself into a very formal pose. "Unfortunately, it is not," he announced in a voice that carried across the courtyard. "I cannot allow you to be engaged to Crown Princess Adale without first challenging you to single combat for the right."

"What?" cried Adale. At the same moment, the little waiting lady made a sudden move, as though she meant to lunge at Theodoar and tear his throat out. But Esofi's parasol shot out and caught her across the chest before she could take even a step.

"Single combat?" repeated Esofi. She gave a small laugh. "Do you think I am some silly courtesan who has come to your country on a whim? My parents signed my marriage contract when I was three years old. Do you think Their Majesties will care what the result of your game is?"

"I have made my challenge," said Theodoar. "You may choose your weapon, or your champion."

"This is not happening," insisted Adale. "Theodoar! What are you thinking?"

"I'm doing this for you, Adale." He looked at her in surprise. "I thought that this was what you wanted."

"I don't *know* what I want!" cried Adale.

"What is he talking about?" asked Esofi, finally acknowledging her.

"I..." Adale found that she didn't know how to begin explaining. "It's...it is complicated. But never mind that now. I will fight for you."

"You certainly will not!" snarled the littlest waiting lady, shoving herself forward so that she and Adale were practically chest to chest, or perhaps chest to stomach. "Princess, I will fight for you, and I will kill this insolent toad where he stands."

"It is not meant to be a fight to the death!" cried Adale.

"Enough," said Esofi, and even though she did not raise her voice, something in her tone compelled them all to silence. "Lord Theodoar, tell me the laws of single combat in your country."

Theodoar nodded, though one eye was locked on Esofi's murderous waiting lady. "It is a straightforward affair, and, as the crown princess said, only until the drawing of first blood, or until someone surrenders. You may fight using a weapon of your choosing. If you win, you may sign the marriage contract with the crown princess uncontested. If you do not, you will pursue her hand no longer."

Adale knew that not even Theodoar believed that last part, but at least now she understood his plan. Winning the duel would delay the marriage proceedings long enough for them to escape the castle, assuming he was able to defeat whomever Esofi selected. Though Theodoar was unquestionably gifted with a sword, Adale had no doubt that the waiting lady was more than capable of murdering him, and might even be proud to be arrested for it.

"Very well," said Esofi, and handed her parasol to Adale.

"What are you doing?" Adale sputtered.

"I am accepting this challenge," said Esofi, as though it was obvious or even logical.

"Yourself?" For the first time, Theodoar looked uncertain. "Surely you wish to select a champion. Or...at least...a different dress."

"Nonsense," said Esofi. "Best to get this over and done with now. Are there any other rules I ought to know about?"

Theodoar seemed uncomfortable, and Adale wondered if his common sense had finally caught up with him. "Only to fight with honor, Princess."

"Then I am ready," said Esofi.

"You must have a weapon," Theodoar began, but before he had even finished the sentence, there was a flash like lightning and a cloud of sparkling rose-pink mist crackled to life around Esofi's hands.

Cries of shock and amazement echoed around the lawn, but Esofi seemed not to hear them. She was already striding forward to meet Theodoar at the middle of the lawn, the pink light trailing up her arms.

Theodoar edged back as if rethinking his challenge, but his friends called out encouragements. Whether this was because they honestly believed he had a chance or simply because they wanted to see a good fight was unclear to Adale.

Theodoar seemed to be cheered by the support, though. He unsheathed his blade and took his position.

"Is this allowed?" murmured Lethea in Adale's ear.

"I didn't know she had magic," Adale whispered back. She realized that she was still clutching at the parasol Esofi had handed her. "Did you know she had magic?"

"I don't know anything," said Lethea with refreshing honesty. "I just turn up for meals."

"Of course she has magic, you fools," hissed Lexandrie. "Did you truly believe she was just a fat little rosebud?"

"Maybe," said Adale. Lexandrie made a noise of disgust and gave her a withering glare.

Movement caught Adale's eye, and she realized that the light in Esofi's right hand was shaping itself into a sword, glittering and translucent. Theodoar looked relieved at the sight; it was clear he believed that Esofi would engage him normally—or, at least, as normally as one could with a sword made of what seemed to be pure magic.

The match began. Theodoar moved in to strike, but Esofi brought her blade up to meet his, parrying the blow. Adale could not see her footwork through her long, elaborate skirts, but she suspected from her stance alone that Esofi had never actually been trained with a sword.

But perhaps she didn't need to be.

Theodoar pulled his sword arm in and stepped back, only to move in again with a complicated three-step attack that Adale had seen him use to best many opponents in the past. Esofi looked surprised, and for a moment, Adale believed the match would be over before it began.

And that was when Esofi swung with her left hand, sending a wave of sparkling light directly at Theodoar. It caught him in the chest and sent him staggering backward. The spectators behind him scattered, but Theodoar regained his footing and moved into a defensive position.

"That's not f—" Theodoar managed to say before another blast of magic hit him. This time, he was not so lucky. The magic knocked him flat on his back.

"Not *fair*!?"

Adale had no idea that the princess could shout like that. It was so at odds with her soft appearance. Esofi stormed toward him, translucent sword still glimmering in her hand, beads of sweat falling from her forehead and distorting her makeup. "You spoiled, selfish, pathetic child! You neglect your lands and your people in order to drink away your inheritance and believe you have the right to face me in combat? I slew three dragons by my own hand during the journey to Birsgen, and I would have killed more if they hadn't learned to fear my scent!"

Another man might have surrendered there, but Theodoar was nothing if not stubborn. In a single lightning-quick movement, he managed to leap back to his feet, sword still in hand. Adale was relieved to see that the magic did not seem to have burned his skin in any way, and Theodoar merely looked as though he had faced an inordinately strong wind.

Theodoar's feet moved automatically into a defensive stance, leaving Adale to wonder how he intended to protect against another wall of pure force. He seemed to reach the same conclusion, though, and stepped forward again to strike.

This time, Esofi brought both hands up in front of herself, palms flat. Before the blade could touch her, a wall of pink light sprang up in front of it. There was a sound like metal striking glass, but Theodoar did not step back the way Adale had been anticipating. Instead he tried the move again, striking at the barrier in the exact same way as though he hoped to shatter it. There was no result.

Not to be dissuaded just yet, Theodoar went to strike a third time. Esofi's hands shifted again, and now Adale could see that there did seem to be a sort of technique to her movements, though it was nothing like the light, rapid art of swordplay. Esofi moved as she breathed, with slow and deliberate gestures that seemed to come from deep within her chest.

As Theodoar's blade came down, the barrier vanished as though it had never been. But before the blade could pierce her, Esofi brought one leg back so that she was almost-kneeling on the grass. At the same time, she drew her right hand upward. Her magical blade intercepted Theodoar's metal one, and there was a sound like a pair of shears cutting through empty air. As one, the spectators gasped.

Half of Theodoar's blade now lay on the fresh morning grass. The other half was still clutched in his hand.

"Do you yield?" asked Esofi.

It seemed a foregone conclusion, but to Adale's great surprise, Theodoar said nothing. Adale wondered if he truly meant to continue the challenge with half a blade. Esofi seemed to have come to the same realization and, before Theodoar could strike again, hit him in the face with another wave of force.

Theodoar hit the grass again on his back, and the broken hilt fell from his hand. He reached for it, but this time, Esofi followed him. Esofi gave a strong kick, and her long skirts prevented Adale from seeing precisely what happened, but Theodoar gave a yelp of pain in response. A moment later, Adale saw him draw his hand close to the safety of his body.

"I didn't mean—" began Theodoar, trying to prop himself up on his elbows. Esofi whipped her arm around, and he found himself staring down at the end of her magical blade.

"I did not order you to speak!" she declared in a voice that reminded Adale of her own parents. She lifted her head to glare at the crowd that had gathered to watch. "There! Has this waste of my time satisfied you? Am I worthy to be your queen and save your country yet, or is there another silly test I must first pass? Tell me quickly!"

Nobody spoke, though a few of the young nobles who had been fortunate enough to get positions near the back of the crowd took the opportunity to sneak away.

"No," said Theodoar at long last. "There is...there is nothing else."

Adale decided to try to reason with Esofi, for Theodoar's sake. After waiting a moment to make sure Esofi wasn't going to start swinging again, Adale moved forward.

"Eso—Princess, I swear, I didn't mean for this to—" Adale began.

"And you!" Esofi looked Adale in the face for the first time, and it was only then that Adale realized that there were tears brimming in her eyes.

"Esofi—"

"No," said Esofi, shaking her head. "I believed...but you must think me quite foolish."

"That's not true!" Adale protested vehemently. "I swear by the deity of your choosing that I knew nothing of this!"

"Do not do me the dishonor of lying to me." Esofi's voice was suddenly very soft. Her ladies gathered around her like a living shield, and the magic vanished from her hands, leaving behind no trace that it had ever been there. "Your mastery of deceit is so poor. How silly of me to be blind to it until now."

"Esofi, I..." There was so, so much that Adale wished to say, but she barely knew how to begin. "I did not want this."

"There seem to be many things you do not want, Crown Princess," retorted Esofi bitterly. "Unfortunately, they have been granted to you regardless."

"Do not say that," pleaded Adale. "Please—walk with me and I will explain. I only need time to find the words—"

Esofi shook her head. "No. No more words. I understand more than you could ever explain."

"Are you all quite finished?" demanded a harsh voice. Adale spun around to discover her own mother standing there, attended by her own ladies and a selection of the castle guards. Her face was flushed scarlet and her braid was half-unpinned. It looked as though she'd run directly from the throne room to the lawn, except that was impossible because Queen Saski did not run.

"Theodoar of Leikr," said Queen Saski, looking more displeased than Adale had seen her in living memory. "On your feet."

Theodoar scrambled upward, and a few of his braver friends stepped forward to help him. When he was properly upright, Queen Saski spoke again.

"I am struggling to think of a reason why I should not have you imprisoned for the rest of your life. Certainly no one would miss you."

"Your Majesty—" he began.

"But then, perhaps that would be too lenient," Queen Saski continued as though he had not spoken. "After all, you are so fond of idleness. I do not think the dungeons would be too dissimilar from the life to which you are accustomed. Perhaps instead I will send you to join the defense of the north, so your existence might benefit someone, even if it is only a hungry dragon."

Theodoar seemed to realize there was nothing he could possibly say to quell her rage.

"I have tolerated you and your shameful, idle peers in my castle in the hopes that your parents might be able to better tend to their lands without you getting underfoot, but now I see that I have merely been rewarding them for their reprehensible parenting," continued Queen Saski. "You will go to your rooms immediately and begin your preparations for the journey home. A carriage will be readied for you by tonight. If I see your face again before my dying day, I will have you thrown into the dungeons for treason. Am I understood?"

Theodoar bowed his head. "Yes, Your Majesty." He cast one last sorrowful look at Adale and then began the walk back to the castle.

"Good." Saski turned her attention to Esofi. "Princess."

"My sincerest apologies, Your Majesty," said Esofi, dabbing at her eyes with a handkerchief embroidered in roses. "If you will grant me but a moment to compose myself." One of her ladies began pulling brushes and face powder from her satchel and set to work repairing Esofi's makeup.

"The rest of you, find your entertainment elsewhere!" ordered Queen Saski, waving a dismissive arm at the spectators that remained. "Or I will send you home to your parents as well!"

The crowd dispersed in record time, leaving only Adale, Lethea, Esofi, and her ladies standing on the grass.

"Now then," said Queen Saski. "I should like to understand precisely what happened here, if you do not mind."

"I mean no disrespect, but there is little to explain, Your Majesty," said Esofi, who looked considerably better than she had a moment ago, though not nearly as picturesque as she'd been when Adale had first encountered her at breakfast. "It was a foolish endeavor, and of no consequence."

Queen Saski seemed to hesitate. "Of no consequence?" Was that hope in her voice? Adale was not entirely certain.

"Of course," said Esofi. "I allowed myself to be drawn into a childish argument, nothing more. I hope you can forgive my misconduct and for drawing you away from your petitioners."

"Of course." Queen Saski spoke very slowly. Adale marveled that her mother appeared to have lost her footing, metaphorically speaking. If only Adale had paid more attention to her tutors as they'd explained the political situation between Ieflaria and Rhodia. Maybe then she'd have some idea of what was going on.

Esofi nodded in satisfaction. "Good. Then let us put the incident out of our minds. There is still so much to accomplish, after all. But I fear I am no longer presentable." Esofi patted her ruined curls. "If you will excuse me? I should not like to appear at my own betrothal looking as I do."

Queen Saski granted her a nod, and Esofi immediately departed, leaving Adale there alone with only Lethea for protection. Once the princess was gone, the last thin traces of pleasantness vanished from Queen Saski's face.

"Are you simple?" her mother hissed at her. "What were you thinking? I should cast you out with Theodoar! You could have destroyed the marriage negotiations! I realize you care nothing for that, but I'd think the lives of your friends would at least hold some value to you!"

"I had no idea that this was Theodoar's plan!" Adale protested weakly. "And nobody knew that the princess had magic!"

Queen Saski pressed a hand to her forehead and spoke in a tone of disbelief. "You didn't know she had—? Why do you think she is here, you fool?"

"To marry someone!" cried Adale. She realized she was still clutching Esofi's parasol, the soft lace pressing patterns into her palms. "To marry me!"

"Have you retained a single word your tutors have said to you?" demanded Queen Saski, continuing as though Adale had not spoken. "The royal family of Rhodia boasts the most gifted mages on the continent of Thiyra! You are lucky she has far greater self-restraint than you do or Theodoar might be dead! Our country will be utterly consumed without her aid, and you have insulted her so gravely that I would not half blame her for returning home immediately! What do you have to say for yourself, Adale?"

Adale looked away from her mother and managed to catch one last glimpse of Esofi's retreating back before she vanished inside the castle walls.

"I'm sorry," she said.

Chapter Three

ESOFI

Once she had made it back to the safety of her rooms, Esofi washed off her makeup until her face was bright and pink. Then she removed her hairpins, allowing her curls to fall in a messy cloud. Finally, she removed her dress, loosened the lacing on her corset, and climbed into bed.

The use of her magic should not have been enough to drain her, but she felt exhausted regardless. It had been this way ever since they had come into Ieflaria—the magic seemed reluctant to come to her now, and when it arrived, it was weak and awkward and slow to respond to her commands. Lexandrie had noticed it as well, and so had Henris and the battlemages. At the time, Esofi had hoped it was merely a side effect of being on the road for so many months, but now she knew better. Ieflaria had offended Talcia so greatly that it was not simply devoid of her magic; it repelled it.

And beneath her physical exhaustion was a deep, persistent ache in her heart.

Stupid, she admonished herself. *Did you think she cared anything for you? This is a political arrangement. Nothing more.*

Still, she had hoped...

Her thoughts went back to Albion. Theirs would have been a marriage of convenience too, but Esofi had always believed that they would quickly come to regard each other with a genuine and maybe even passionate love.

Maybe. But then, maybe not. Perhaps I was lying to myself about that, too.

Esofi pressed her face into her pillow. Was she really so repugnant that Adale would arrange a duel in order to delay their wedding? Even if that nobleman had managed to defeat her, surely they hadn't been foolish enough to believe that Their Majesties would simply accept it and throw away almost a decade and a half of careful planning?

Adale must have been truly desperate to even try.

Tears sprung to Esofi's eyes, which only made her angrier with herself, which in turn led to more tears. Adale hadn't even given her a chance! They'd spoken only twice, and yet the crown princess had already decided that she would rather spend her life as an untitled vagrant than marry Esofi!

"I'm not as bad as that," whispered Esofi to herself. "Someone would have told me if I was." Probably. Her sisters, certainly. Or her mother. They had never hesitated to point out her flaws. Surely, someone would have mentioned it by now if she was unbearable, even if it was only in passing.

Her pillow was wet, and so Esofi flipped it over, savoring the coolness on her cheek. She began to hum a common Rhodian hymn to Talcia, lazy fingertips tracing the designs woven into her blankets.

"I do not need her love," Esofi reminded herself. "I already have so much." And that was true. She had her own waiting ladies, who had yet to fail her in even the smallest task. She had the promise from Their Majesties that had been added to the marriage contract just yesterday. And, most importantly, she had the blessing of her goddess.

Esofi wondered if Adale had reviewed the contract and seen the addition yet but then reminded herself that she did not care. To be honest, Adale probably did not care much either. Esofi was still not completely convinced that Adale would even be at the signing that afternoon. Even though Theodoar had lost the duel, there was still a chance that Adale would try to make her escape before her freedom was signed away forever.

Esofi tried to imagine Adale hastily fitting everything she owned into a few small traveling bags, stopping now and again to check the hour. It was depressingly easy to visualize, and Esofi hoped that this was simply a result of her overactive imagination and not a true vision from Talcia. But then, Talcia had never sent her a vision before, and Esofi doubted that she would begin now.

And so what if it was true? So what if Adale was packing her things as even now Esofi lay there feeling sorry for herself? Let her leave! Esofi wouldn't even ask Their Majesties to send guards after their wayward daughter. She would simply accept the hand of whatever nobleman or woman was next in line and never think upon this day again.

"I do not care," Esofi whispered to herself. "I've no reason to care."

Esofi closed her eyes and eventually drifted off to sleep. She had a brief, absurd dream that her parents arrived from Rhodia and demanded to know who she would be marrying. When she told them that she was not entirely certain yet, they suggested she give up her title and become a miller instead, a prospect which upset Esofi so badly that she awoke with a start.

The sun was low in the sky, casting shades of gold across the courtyard. Esofi sat upright in her bed and saw that Lexandrie was sitting in the soft chair across from her, reading a book.

"I have missed the betrothal," said Esofi. It was not a question. "Why did you not wake me?"

Lexandrie glanced up for the briefest of moments. "You needed the rest, and the Ieflarians needed to be shown they could not insult you without consequence."

Esofi's feet found the carpet. "Had you asked, I would not have—"

"And that is why I did not ask," retorted Lexandrie. "You are the future queen of Ieflaria. Try to have some pride."

"Lexandrie, the marriage contract!"

"It will keep until tomorrow!" Lexandrie snapped her book shut and stood. "Don't you dare act as though I've spoiled your plans. You know Their Majesties are desperate to have you as their daughter-in-law! You could skip through the streets of Birsgen with a teapot on your head and they would still let you marry Adale! Why do you refuse to take advantage of your position?"

"Because I already have everything I require," said Esofi. "And demanding favors for the sake of favors will endear me to nobody."

"I'm not talking about favors! I'm talking about respect!"

"I would say I already earned their respect this morning!"

Lexandrie didn't seem to know how to respond to that. "Well, you certainly took your time of it," she muttered at last, but most of the fire had gone from her. "You'll take dinner in your rooms tonight. Let them wonder a bit more. Tomorrow, you may do as you like."

"Very well," said Esofi, who had not been looking forward to being gawked at during the evening meal in any case. "Has there been any news?"

"Nothing of importance, I think." Lexandrie shrugged. "But Lisette has been about. She could tell you better than I."

"You let Lisette leave?" cried Esofi, suddenly feeling quite sick.

"As though I could have stopped her!" Lexandrie rolled her eyes. "Worry not, she has killed nobody, or if she has, they have not yet discovered the body."

"I would like to speak with her," said Esofi. "Immediately, if at all possible."

Lexandrie sighed as though Esofi had given a near-impossible order but left the room without an argument. Esofi went to the wardrobe and began to search for her dressing gown. With the setting of the sun, the castle had grown significantly colder.

By the time Lisette arrived, Esofi was wrapped in her robe and sitting in the chair that Lexandrie had vacated. Lisette regarded Esofi rather coolly.

"What are they saying?" asked Esofi.

Lisette crossed her arms. "The foolish ones wonder if you will return to Rhodia. Others ask if you will marry one of the children of the king's brother instead of the crown princess. I think they deserve to wonder."

That sounded very much like what Lexandrie had said, and Esofi wondered if they'd discussed it at some point. "Is the crown princess still in the castle?"

"Yes," said Lisette. "After all that trouble, she chose not to flee, though she certainly had her chance. Most unusual."

"Mm," said Esofi. "What do you make of her?"

Lisette shrugged. "She is a child, just as her companions are. But at least she will not get in your way."

"She did not ever expect to rule," noted Esofi. "If Albion had lived, she could have dedicated her entire life to hunting and drinking. I think she resents the sudden responsibility."

"Perhaps," said Lisette, glancing away. "But that does not excuse her behavior."

"No," agreed Esofi. "It does not."

About an hour later, servants arrived with food. Esofi and her ladies had their meal in the sitting room, something that Esofi quickly realized she enjoyed. It would not be appropriate to never appear for a meal again, but right then, she needed to be away from prying eyes and it would be good to know she had the option again in the future, should she need it.

The servants took the dishes and small collapsible tables away when the meal was finished, and Esofi contemplated simply going back to bed. Her magic was restored, but she still felt oddly empty. Perhaps attending the evening service would make her feel better. But that would require her to dress again...

Esofi glanced around at her ladies. Lexandrie was reading again, though her eyes seemed a bit glazed over, and Mireille was picking at her embroidery. The mood in the room was warm and lazy, and Esofi knew she'd only get groans of protest if she announced her intention to go to a service.

Esofi settled back against the couch and closed her eyes, just to rest them. She might have fallen asleep for just a moment, but soon enough, a knock at the door pulled her awake.

"Someone get that," mumbled Esofi. As usual, Mireille was the one to rise. She opened the door and released a small gasp.

"Oh," said Mireille. "Crown Princess!"

Esofi came back to full awakening at the words. Lexandrie's eyes snapped open as well, her expression twisting into one of rage. Adale spoke, but Esofi could not make out the words.

"I am sorry, but she is resting," said Mireille firmly.

"I understand," Adale sighed. "Will you at least give her this, then?"

"Very well." Mireille sounded a little confused. "Well, good night—"

"Wait," said Adale. "Will she be at breakfast tomorrow?"

"I could not guess, Crown Princess," Mireille responded. "Good night."

The door closed, and Mireille came back. She was holding a very small basket with a soft cloth draped over the top.

"What's that, Mireille?" asked Lexandrie.

"I do not know yet," said Mireille, sitting down beside Esofi. "Pastries, perhaps?"

"As though Esofi needs any more of those," muttered Lexandrie.

"What?" Lisette hurried over, looking displeased. "Don't eat anything until I've—"

Esofi reached over and pulled the fabric away, and Mireille gasped. Curled up in the basket was a flat-faced, cream-colored kitten. It gave the tiniest cry of protest as it lifted its head to sniff at its new surroundings.

"Oh, for the love of—" began Lisette in disgust. "She truly is a child!"

Esofi picked up the kitten carefully, making sure not to let its claws catch on the fabric of her robe. It seemed to be of a good temperament with a fine seal-point pattern offsetting the large fluff of pale fur. It was not so small that Esofi thought it would need to be bottle-fed and seemed to be well-bred. Esofi wondered if Adale had purchased it from a breeder and if the princess might give her the name. She was completely unfamiliar with this Ieflarian breed and hoped it did not require some manner of special treatment.

"You're not going to keep it, are you?" asked Lexandrie hopelessly.

"Well, I'm not going to turn him out," reasoned Esofi, rubbing her finger against the kitten's little face.

"We'll have fur everywhere," moaned Lexandrie. "It will claw at the furniture and shred our dresses—and besides, accepting the gift means you've forgiven her."

"I have forgiven her," said Esofi. "She cannot help her nature." The kitten pressed up against her décolletage, and Esofi allowed him to stay there. "Or did you mean for me to hate her forever?"

"Not forever," said Lexandrie. "Just until she is well and truly sorry. No more than a year."

Esofi sighed. "I said I have forgiven her, not that I trust her. But to be angry with her now would only exhaust me. We are going to be together for a very long time, and I would like for it to be pleasant if at all possible. Perhaps she is hoping for the same thing."

"I don't like it," sulked Lexandrie. "Why has she suddenly decided she wants to court you? Why did she not come to that realization before prompting one of her friends to challenge you in public? It defies reason."

"I do not know," admitted Esofi. "Perhaps tomorrow we can speak, and she will tell me for herself."

"Or perhaps she is merely a fool," Lisette suggested dryly.

"Yes, you have all made your opinions known." Esofi sighed. "I don't suppose there's a note in the basket?"

"Only dishes," reported Mireille, withdrawing two silver bowls, one for food and the other for water. "We'll have to get the servants to bring sand, if you truly do mean to keep it."

"I do," said Esofi, running her hand along the kitten's almost comically fluffy tail. "I suppose I must also think of a name."

"Is it a male or a female?" asked Mireille.

"A male, I think," Esofi said. "But I am not entirely certain. Why did she not leave a note?"

"Perhaps she is illiterate," suggested Lexandrie, who had now taken a seat as far away from Esofi as she could get without actually leaving the room.

"I very much doubt that," said Esofi. "But even if she did not wish to apologize, I would have liked more information about the breeder."

"Perhaps it is part of her plan to get you to speak with her again," suggested Mireille. "She said she wanted to see you at breakfast tomorrow. I think she may be worried that she has lost your heart forever."

"But why does she suddenly want it?" mused Esofi. "That is the true question, is it not?"

"Perhaps she is only pretending," said Lexandrie flatly. "Perhaps her mother has threatened her if she does not win you."

Esofi glared. "And that would be the only reason for someone trying to win me, wouldn't it?"

"I didn't say that!" Lexandrie protested. "I am only being realistic, since you seem determined to make everything so romantic! I find it far more likely that Their Majesties have told her she will be disinherited if she loses you!"

"They would not do that to their only remaining child," said Esofi.

"You don't know that!" cried Lexandrie. "You have only seen of them what they've allowed you to see! For all we know, they could be cruel or vicious or—"

"Lexandrie, enough," said Esofi firmly. "I am too tired for bickering."

"Fine!" Lexandrie got up. "I am withdrawing for the evening. Good night to you all!" She stormed from the room, slamming the door behind her.

"She's not angry at you, but on your behalf," Mireille assured her. "Worry not. Tomorrow her attitude will have improved; I am certain of it." She reached over to pet the kitten again, babbling nonsense at him and trying to coax another soft mew out. "What should we name him? Creme? Sugar?" Mireille smiled brightly. "But that sounds as though I mean to eat him."

"Give me until morning," said Esofi. "If something has not come to me by then, you may pick the name." Mireille's face lit at the declaration. Esofi scratched the kitten behind the ears and felt a gentle rumbling from deep within his throat.

"Good night, then, Princess," Mireille said, rubbing the kitten's little face once more. "I think we will all feel better after a good night's rest."

She got up and left the room as Lexandrie had, though this time it involved no slamming of doors. Esofi thought of her own waiting bed and rose to her feet.

Perhaps it was only because she was too tired to dwell too deeply on it, but she seemed to feel just a little bit less hurt.

Esofi awoke the next morning with the kitten asleep on her face. She carefully lifted him away, which got a few squeaks of annoyance, and set him back down on the opposite pillow.

Esofi was not yet sure how her failure to sign the contract yesterday would affect her schedule. She'd really been hoping to take a tour of Birsgen's medical facilities today. The court mage had explained to her that the Ieflarians had turned to strange practices in order to give medical care. The court mage had called it "science," which Esofi didn't like the sound of at all.

But if Their Majesties summoned her to sign the agreement, she might have to put off the tour, and that was not something Esofi wanted to do.

The court mage was an Ieflarian man named Arran Eads, who seemed to be trying to make the best of an impossible situation. Officially, he was meant to be the liaison between the Temple of Talcia and the royal court. In Esofi's opinion, he had not been properly educated and, therefore, could not really be relied upon in the same way she could Henris or any of the court mages back home. He was still one of the most powerful Ieflarian mages in existence, but that really wasn't saying much. Neither of his two apprentices seemed to be particularly skilled either.

Archmage Eads didn't actually spend much time worrying about magic, though. When he'd spoken to Esofi, he'd tried to tell her some nonsense about how they'd started telling the peasants to boil water and this had somehow done something to decrease the rate of sickness and infection. None of it made any sense, and it honestly sounded like desperate superstition.

The battlemages really were Esofi's first priority, and she was scheduled to meet again with Their Majesties' military commanders to discuss their placement, but she knew better than to neglect the healers entirely. That day, she would go to the Temple of Adranus and see precisely what was going on there.

Adranus was the God of Death first and foremost, so it confused Esofi to learn that he was associated so strongly with healing in Ieflaria. Back home, he was restricted to his domain of Death, and healing came from his daughter, Adalia. But apparently, Adalia's name was not so well known here, and it was the priests of Adranus who had turned to other avenues in order to tend to the sick and dying. Archmage Eads had used such strange words: surgery, bacteria, sterilization.

In Esofi's opinion, it was edging near to blasphemy. Taking fate into one's own hands was particularly ill-advised, and only time would tell if Esofi would be forced to order the entire temple to be shut down. Hopefully, it would not come to that. She had a feeling the priests meant well and weren't even aware they had strayed so far from the path of righteousness.

Perhaps after they had fixed the magical situation in Ieflaria, she could focus her attentions on encouraging the people to return to relying upon healing magic, rather than confusing nonsense. Hopefully, it wouldn't be too difficult. Despite her strong convictions, she didn't want to make enemies of anyone, not even the priests of Adranus.

Esofi put those worries out of her mind and dressed for the day. She wore a slightly more elaborate dress than she'd been choosing for the past few days. She was already growing tired of the dreary attire worn by the Ieflarian people, mourning or not. And for some reason, which might or might not have been related to the duel yesterday, she felt like being impressive. The gown she selected was a bright sky-blue color, with layers of lace and ruffles drawing emphasis to the sleeves, bust, and skirt. Her ladies wove silk flowers into her curls, which were pinned up.

Finally, when she was ready, they departed to take their breakfast in the banquet hall, as usual. Esofi had a feeling that Crown Princess Adale would be waiting for them there, as she seemed eager to win Esofi's forgiveness for reasons that were not entirely clear yet.

Her instincts were correct. Upon entering the room, Esofi's focus went to the spot beside the seats where Their Majesties would sit. Adale was waiting there, looking slightly on edge. It was a stark contrast to her waiting lady, who was all but asleep. When Adale saw Esofi, her entire face brightened.

Esofi took her usual seat on the other side of the table, next to where Queen Saski would sit. The room was not quite crowded yet, but she knew it would be very soon.

"Esofi—" began Adale. "Princess, did you receive—?"

"The basket? Yes," said Esofi evenly, ignoring how her ladies glared.

"Oh," said Adale. "Well. Did you like him? Because if you didn't—"

"I did," Esofi replied. "Very much."

"Oh," said Adale again. "Well...good. I'm glad to hear it."

Esofi gave a small nod.

"Would you be willing to walk with me today?" asked Adale. Lisette gave a soft growl at the suggestion.

"Perhaps I would," said Esofi. "However, I have agreed to visit the Temple of Adranus today, and cannot yet say if I will have the time."

"Please," said Adale, surprising Esofi with the quiet desperation in her voice and her face. "Just an hour. Or less. Half an hour. I just—"

"Very well," said Esofi, deciding to be merciful and cut off Adale's babblings. "But no more than half an hour. I cannot be late."

At those words, Adale looked as though a weight had been lifted from her, but before she could say anything more, the doors opened and King Dietrich and Queen Saski entered the hall. All conversation ceased as Their Majesties took their seats, and the servants hurried out to serve the meal.

"Princess," said Queen Saski in a pained voice. "We were so disappointed to hear you had fallen ill last night. I sent a healer, but your waiting lady turned him away. I hope you are better today?"

"Yes, I believe so," replied Esofi. "I was just telling Adale that I hope to visit the Temple of Adranus today. I have heard such...curious things about it."

Queen Saski seemed reluctant to acknowledge her own daughter, as though she was afraid that Esofi would interpret it as Saski supporting Adale's actions of the previous day. Esofi did not comment on it, however, and kept the conversation light and cheerful, if not a bit strained.

Several times, Saski did attempt to steer the conversation in the direction of the betrothal, but Esofi was ready for her.

She only had to point at a random dish on the table and ask, "What is that called?" in a voice loud enough to be heard by everyone in the room, and the subject would immediately turn to the dish, its history, and which region of Ieflaria made it best.

Esofi knew she could not put off the signing of the marriage contract forever, though. Sooner or later, Their Majesties would require her to name a day.

At long last, the meal came to an end. The servants emerged again to clear the dishes away, and Esofi waited until they were done before she rose and walked out of the room at a lazy, unhurried pace. Adale seemed not to know whether she ought to approach her or wait to be summoned. In truth, Esofi was not sure what she preferred.

The day seemed to be fair, and so Esofi began walking in the direction of the gardens. Adale hurried to meet her pace so that they were side by side, their hands occasionally brushing against each other for the briefest of moments. The footsteps of her ladies sounded behind Esofi, their presence simultaneously reassuring and irritating.

The gardens, fortunately, were not crowded just yet, though Esofi had a faint suspicion that some of the nobles and servants hadn't decided to venture outside until they'd seen the princesses leaving. Court life was the same, no matter the country. It was almost impossible to ever be truly alone.

"I wanted to apologize properly," said Adale at last as they walked through an avenue of hedges. "I know you have no reason to believe me, but I swear I did not ask Theodoar to challenge you."

"But you asked him something," said Esofi, pausing in her stride.

"I didn't..." Adale stopped walking as well. She looked defeated. "No. You are right. I did. I just...I never thought that he would bring you into it."

"How could that be?" questioned Esofi.

"I thought we would just be able to leave without calling any attention to ourselves," explained Adale. "Just...slip away in the night."

Esofi pressed her lips together.

"It wasn't because of you!" cried Adale. "Please, even if you don't believe anything else I have to say, at least listen to this. I do not find you unappealing."

"Then why?" asked Esofi.

"Ieflaria does not deserve me." Adale shook her head. "And neither do you. I could not make you happy, and I certainly would not make a good queen. I thought perhaps you would be engaged to someone more suitable in my place, someone who could give you what you needed."

"Why are you so certain that you wouldn't?" asked Esofi.

Adale shrugged. "I know myself. There's no sense in lying. You told Theodoar that he was a child, that he was selfish, and...and all those other things you said. I am no different. If anything, I am worse."

"Do you not believe you have the capacity for change?" asked Esofi.

"I do not know," admitted Adale. "When I think of ruling, I feel sick. I can't breathe and all I want to do is run away because one wrong decision could ruin everything for thousands of people, and I'm very, very good at making wrong decisions!" Her voice broke on the last word.

"You don't think I'm not afraid too?" asked Esofi softly. "To be afraid to rule a nation is not cowardice. It is common sense."

"But you'd do it anyway?" asked Adale.

"It is my responsibility," said Esofi. "Perhaps things work differently in Ieflaria. It seems only the eldest siblings strive to be worthy of their titles, while the younger ones are allowed to spend their days in idleness. It is as though you are unaware what could befall—" She stopped short, horrified, as she realized too late that Adale knew all too well what could befall a firstborn.

But Adale shook her head. "No. You're right."

"I did not mean—" Esofi began.

"You're right," Adale repeated firmly. "We've been fortunate. We haven't had a plague in ages. We haven't fought a war since we declared independence, and that was hardly a war at all. We've had so many people blessed with Eyvindr's magic that we could probably salt our fields and still get a good harvest. The dragons have been a problem, but we don't usually lose our heirs, and the nobility has been prosperous enough that they can afford to let their younger children run wild. Things were good for so long that I think we forgot it could be any other way."

Esofi looked at her searchingly. "Why did you not run when you had the chance?"

"I can't explain it," said Adale. "It's just...the duel, and you, and my cousins, and... I'm so terrible at explaining myself. I must seem like a babbling child." Adale pressed her hands to her forehead. "Where to even begin?"

Esofi said nothing.

"I suppose...the night before the duel. When I met you after the hunt. I wanted to tell you then that I was leaving, and you could marry one of my cousins instead. But when I saw you, I couldn't. And so I left it to Theodoar. And of course he..." Adale shook her head. "I love him, but he is such a fool."

Esofi swallowed. *You love him?* She wanted to ask, but she did not. Those were questions for Lisette's mouth, not Esofi's.

"You must understand. I wasn't raised the same way you were. I always thought I would be allowed a say in who I married. The idea of an arranged betrothal is frightening to me, even now."

"But you are a princess!" Esofi was incredulous. "Making an advantageous marriage is one of your responsibilities—one of your apparently *very few* responsibilities." Esofi knew she was being rude, but Adale didn't seem to mind the insult.

"Haven't you ever been in love?" asked Adale.

Esofi was taken aback, and she raised her head defiantly. "What does *that* have to do with anything?"

"Wouldn't you like to be in love with the one you marry?" Adale pressed.

"Well, yes," said Esofi. "I suppose. Yes. If at all possible. But most couples of our station are married first, and grow to love one another afterward with Pemele's guidance."

"Some might be afraid to take such a risk." Adale scuffed her shoe into the stone pathway awkwardly.

"Is it because you are in love with someone else already?" asked Esofi.

"Gods, no, Esofi!" Adale pressed her hands to her forehead. Her face began slowly turning red. "Is that what you think?"

"You just told me that you love Theodoar," said Esofi.

"I do love Theodoar," agreed Adale. "I love him as I loved Albion. But I am not in love with him. Is that what you thought?"

Esofi bit her lip and said nothing.

"I have been worried about you," said Adale, her silver eyes staring into Esofi's. "When your ladies told us that you wouldn't be able to make it to the signing, I was afraid you were planning to leave Ieflaria forever. Then you weren't at dinner, and you didn't go to the evening service—"

"You went to a service?" interrupted Esofi, her eyebrows rising.

"Yes! Well...most of one," said Adale. "I left before the closing rites. They're always so dull! I don't think anyone noticed."

Esofi gave a quiet little sigh.

"My point, though," said Adale, "is you're so...you care so much for Ieflaria already. You only just got here, and you're making all sorts of plans, and everyone's convinced things are going to improve because of the battlemages, and I don't know anything about anything and I've lived here all my life! I know when people talk about me, they say I'm an overgrown child. And it's never bothered me before, not really. But when they talk about you...they say you're going to be our queen. Nobody's ever said that about me."

"Do you want them to?"

"I don't know!" Adale sounded anguished. "I don't know—and even if they did, they would be wrong. I don't know anything. I don't even know what you've added to the marriage contract. I don't know if it says I can never go riding again or drink excessively or if I have to be in by sundown—"

"What," interrupted Esofi, "are you talking about?"

Adale didn't respond right away. She seemed to be trying to catch her breath. "The marriage contract," she said at last. "I know you added something to it. You mentioned it the other night. Something that wasn't in your agreement with Albion."

"And you believe that it is related to your conduct?" Esofi fought to keep her lips from curling into a smile. She wasn't sure if she was successful or not.

"What else would it be?" reasoned Adale.

Esofi sighed. "The addition that was made to the marriage contract had nothing to do with you. If you'd only asked, I would have told you."

Adale's face changed. "What? But then, but then what could possibly be—"

"It was a grant," said Esofi. "A one-time payment of one hundred thousand crowns for the establishment of a university for the teaching of magics, to be managed under the guidance of the Temple of Talcia. The university will also receive an additional ten thousand crowns for every year that follows, for the purpose of salaries and maintenance."

Adale's mouth fell open.

"We have a university in Rhodia, and it has served us well for hundreds of years," Esofi explained, since Adale seemed to be having difficulty with words. "The battlemages I have brought are not immortal. Sooner or later, they will need to be replaced, and some may wish to return home. Constantly importing them from Rhodia would be wasteful when we could educate and hire Ieflarians."

"You got one hundred thousand crowns out of my parents?" Adale whispered.

"It's not spending money!" huffed Esofi. "Have you even been listening to me?"

"I'm listening! I'm not allowed to be impressed now?"

"Well, if you're hoping that I mean to pocket some of it, let me tell you that you are sadly mistaken," said Esofi. "As I indicated to you before, the worship of Talcia has been neglected for far too long in your country. My priority is to completely revitalize her temple here in Birsgen. It's in shameful condition compared to the Temple of Iolar, or so I am told."

"Oh," said Adale.

"I would like the university to be built on the temple grounds as well," continued Esofi. "If there is not enough land, I intend to purchase the surrounding properties in the temple's name."

"Oh," Adale repeated. It seemed to be all she was capable of saying. "Well..."

"I am to visit the Temple of Adranus today," continued Esofi. "I am told it is not far from the Temple of Talcia. So perhaps if the tour does not take up too much of my time, I will be able to speak with the archpriestess of Talcia. I think she will be glad for the news."

"I'm sure she will," said Adale. "And all of our temples are in the same area of the upper city, so it won't be much trouble for you to go directly to Talcia from the hospital."

Esofi nodded. "Yes. The...hospital." She felt her lips press together in dismay at the word, strange and unfamiliar. "I fear the Temple of Adranus may have fallen to heresy. The things I have been told are...troubling, which is why I have chosen to prioritize it over my visit to Talcia's temple. I sincerely hope that we won't have to burn it."

"Well, I think—" began Adale again. Then her brow furrowed. She looked Esofi in the eyes. "I'm sorry, what did you just say?"

"I said, I hope we will not have to burn it," repeated Esofi. "It would be a dreadful waste of resources."

Adale's mouth moved, but no words were forthcoming. Esofi waited politely for the crown princess to formulate a sentence. Finally, Adale said, "Have you spoken to my parents about your...uh, your concerns?"

"No," admitted Esofi. She'd wanted to, especially after speaking to the archmage, but there had been no time. "Not yet. But surely they cannot be oblivious to what is happening."

"Right," said Adale, speaking very slowly. Esofi had the feeling that she was trying to pick her words carefully. "I wonder if I could trouble you to explain exactly what you're worried about? Perhaps with an emphasis on why you believe the hospital needs to be burned?"

"Is it not obvious?" asked Esofi. "The priests of Adranus have rejected their duties as healers. Instead, they have turned to those grotesque practices that your court mage seems so impressed by. Cutting people open with knives and—and talking about tiny invisible creatures and all those other horrible things he told me." Esofi shuddered, and then shook her head. "I cannot imagine Adranus condoning such barbaric practices."

"The Temple of Adranus has made some incredible breakthroughs in the past years," pointed out Adale with a frown. "As I said, we haven't had a plague in... I don't know. Decades. Maybe even a century."

"Hm." Esofi was unconvinced, but she was not in the mood for a fight, or at least not until she spoke to the archpriest and inspected the facility for herself. "Well, I shall make up my mind today."

"Allow me to accompany you, then," said Adale with more than a hint of urgency in her voice. "Please."

Esofi pressed her lips together again. "It is a public establishment and so I can hardly stop you. But I didn't think you cared for matters of theology."

"It's less the theology and more the burning down of important buildings," said Adale. "I apologize if I seem to be harping on the subject, but—"

Esofi rolled her eyes. "You do not think I will act before consulting with Their Majesties, do you? If it is determined that the temple grounds need to be purified—"

"They don't," interrupted Adale.

"Crown Princess, I mean no disrespect, but by your own admission, you cannot even sit through an ordinary evening service," Esofi pointed out. "I hardly think you are qualified to judge."

"And you are?" retorted Adale. "You're not Iolar. You're not Talcia. And you're not Adranus. You've no right to claim your opinions are the same as theirs unless they've told you so themselves."

"We have been granted magic so that we are constantly reminded that our influence upon Inthya is only due to the will of the gods," said Esofi. "To alter the world in other ways is hubris."

"That's ridiculous," said Adale. "We already create so much without the use of magic. Even you don't use magic for everything. If I build a house without the use of magic, am I committing a sin?"

"That is not the same," Esofi said impatiently. "Any peasant can build a house or at least learn how to. It is not some secret knowledge—"

"But why not?" pressed Adale. "Because we already understand it?"

"Yes!" said Esofi.

"But you wrote the new segment of the marriage contract yourself, didn't you?" asked Adale.

"I did. What of it?" asked Esofi suspiciously.

"I could never do that," explained Adale passionately. "I'm terrible with words, and even if I wasn't, I haven't the attention for such things. Writing anything longer than a letter is impossible for me."

"That's nonsense. You just haven't been properly educated—" Esofi began.

"No," interrupted Adale. "I think it's because you've stolen forbidden knowledge or possibly been in contact with demons. Because if I don't understand it, that's the only reasonable explanation and now I must burn you."

Despite herself, Esofi felt a laugh escape her mouth. Adale looked relieved at the sound. Perhaps she'd been expecting Esofi to yell at her instead. And perhaps Esofi had been intending to. She wasn't certain.

"You're right, you know," said Adale after a short pause. "I probably am not qualified to speak about things like...this. But I think...I think if the gods really are watching us, I think they'd be proud of how much we've learned. I don't think they want us to be naked, helpless children living in caves or, or being eaten by dragons."

"I do not know," said Esofi wistfully. "If only they would speak to me, things would be so much easier."

"You seem to be doing well, though," said Adale. "You've already accomplished so much, and once the contract is signed..."

"It may seem that way to you," sighed Esofi. "But...you're not the only one who is afraid. Sometimes I feel like I have no idea what I'm doing. I've had all this training, but it was just that. Training. None of it has been real, until now. I keep expecting someone to announce that I am a fraud, but nobody ever does."

"You killed real dragons, didn't you?" asked Adale.

"Yes," said Esofi. "But that's...that was far more straightforward."

Adale laughed.

"I mean it!" cried Esofi. "And even if I made a mistake, there were always other battlemages who could have stepped in. But treaties and contracts and laws aren't like that. If I make the wrong choice, there will be no one there to protect us. I could doom us all so easily."

"You are not going to doom anyone," said Adale. "I can't believe you could say such a thing about yourself. You're more capable than anyone else our age in the castle! And, and besides, you're not going to be alone. My parents aren't going anywhere, and they have all their advisors, too."

Esofi met Adale's eyes and then looked down at her hands. "You know, though," she said. "You know what I mean."

"Yes," said Adale. "But—but the difference between you and me is you're incredible and I'm hopeless."

Esofi laughed and hit Adale's shoulder, lightly, with her fan. "Don't be ridiculous!" she laughed. "If you were truly hopeless, your parents would not have made you their heir."

"That's complicated," said Adale quietly.

"Listen to me," said Esofi. "Maybe you're not very good at reading and writing and memorizing facts. Maybe you aren't blessed by any of the gods. But that doesn't mean you don't have other skills. Different skills. You only need to identify them."

Adale swallowed. "Well, maybe," she said, but the words came out strangely hoarse. She coughed a few times, as though there was something stuck in her throat. Before Esofi could ask if she was all right, they were interrupted.

"Crown Princess!" A maid was all but running toward them, her maid cap askew. Adale and Esofi both turned to look at her.

"What's the matter, Runa?" Adale asked, stepping forward.

"Forgive my intrusion." Runa curtsied at Esofi, and turned back to Adale. "Crown Princess, I have a message from Her Majesty. She says that you are to report to the throne room immediately to greet the Duke and Duchess of Valenleht."

"Damn it!" cursed Adale. "And their children, too, I take it?"

"I am afraid so, Crown Princess," said the maid.

"The Duke and Duchess of Valenleht?" asked Esofi. The titles sounded familiar, and she searched her memories. "That is...King Dietrich's brother and his wife, is it not?"

"And the twins," grumbled Adale. "My cousins. I know why they're here. I just didn't think they'd be so quick about it." Her hands clenched into fists.

"Oh," said Esofi. "Forgive me, but are these the same cousins that you wished me to consider marrying in your place?"

"By the gods." Adale slapped both hands over her eyes and held them there. "I was hoping you wouldn't pick up on that. Yes."

Esofi felt an awkward tightness in her chest. It seemed quite likely that the twins had come immediately after hearing that it seemed Adale might not be marrying Esofi after all, perhaps to submit themselves as substitute candidates.

And there is nothing wrong with that, Esofi reminded herself. *In fact, it is precisely what Adale had been hoping for.*

But Adale seemed to be in the process of changing her mind. And Esofi...well...she wasn't certain what she wanted just yet.

"But now I must go and see to this." Adale shook her head in disgust. "I apologize, Princess. I wish I could have accompanied you today."

"It is not your fault," said Esofi. She hesitated. "Entirely."

Adale took Esofi's hand and raised it to her lips. The kiss was brief, barely more than a brush, but Esofi felt an odd lurch in her stomach at the gesture. Adale might have also squeezed her hand for just a moment before releasing it, but perhaps that was just Esofi's imagination.

"Does this mean we don't have to go to the temple today after all?" asked Lexandrie hopefully.

Esofi continued to stare down at her glove, as though seeing the ghost of Adale's lips upon it. It was certainly not the first time someone had kissed her hand, but it was the first time she thought that someone might actually care for her in a romantic way.

"Yes," said Esofi at last. For some reason, her own voice sounded odd to her ears. "I suppose it does."

"Here, what's the matter with you?" demanded Lexandrie. "You'd better not be getting stupid about her."

Esofi snapped her head around to glare at her cousin. "What are you talking about?"

"You know what I'm talking about!" Lexandrie glared at Esofi's hand as though she could see the warm spots that Adale's lips and fingertips had left upon it. "You're becoming infatuated simply because you think she might care for you."

"Do not be ridiculous," said Esofi. "It is a great deal more complex than that."

"Don't try to lie to me!" cried Lexandrie. "If she's suddenly decided to act as though she means to court you, it means that she's finally wised up to how much political power—"

"Political power? I am sorry. Are we discussing the same woman?" retorted Esofi.

"And who says she's only acting?" piped up Mireille. "Maybe she truly does care for Esofi."

"You shut up!" Lexandrie snapped.

"I won't!" Mireille seemed to try to raise herself up to Lexandrie's height. She was entirely unsuccessful but seemed to be unaware of the fact. "Why shouldn't the crown princess fall in love with Esofi?"

"Because that's not how it works, you silly girl!"

"Yes," cut in Esofi coldly. "No one could possibly want me simply by virtue of who I am. And she certainly could not want me for my face. The only explanation is that she sees me as a tool to further her own agenda."

"And what's the matter with that?" demanded Lexandrie. "You know that's just the way it is for us."

"No, not for us. Just for me!" cried Esofi. "You've never had any trouble believing that someone found you beautiful! It's only when it comes to me that love is impossible."

"You are in love with her," Lexandrie announced. "Though I cannot imagine why. Surely you are not that desperate. At least meet her cousins first. They might even be proper suitors."

"Of course I will meet them," said Esofi. "You seem to have a rather low opinion of my intelligence right now, but I assure you that I am open to the possibility of either of them attempting to court me. Regardless of what you may think, my priority is still becoming the queen of Ieflaria."

"Good," said Lexandrie. "Because she is not in love with you. She finds you tedious and stifling. And on top of everything, she thinks you're a religious fanatic, or had you forgotten that part already?"

"I find it suspicious and strange that you know the crown princess's mind so well," retorted Esofi. "Have you been meeting with her in secret?"

"I'm only telling you these things because nobody else will," said Lexandrie. "There is no need for you to become so defensive."

"That's not true!" objected Mireille. "Nothing you've said is true! Anyone could love Esofi if they talked to her. You're just, you can't be happy for her, because you're so jealous!"

"*Jealous*!?" Lexandrie practically screamed. "Why would I be jealous of—?"

"Enough!" cried Esofi. "All of you! Especially you, Lexandrie! You may occupy yourself elsewhere if you've nothing civil to say!"

"Fine!" Lexandrie turned around with a flourish. "What should you care for what I have to say when you could spend your days listening to the mindless praise of two girls who only pretend to be ladies?"

"You are dismissed, Lexandrie," said Esofi. Fortunately, Lexandrie seemed to have no more to say and stormed away in the direction of the castle.

"What madness came over her?" wondered Mireille once she had gone. "I've never heard her speak in such a way before."

"It is a strange habit she shares with my mother and sisters," said Esofi bitterly. "She has been so pleasant these past months, I hoped that she left it behind in Rhodia."

"Well, she is wrong," proclaimed Mireille. "I think the crown princess does truly care for you. Why else would she apologize and speak so honestly with you?"

"I would like to believe that as well." Esofi kept her voice quiet, just in case someone was listening. "But I am not without my doubts."

"Even now?" Mireille looked up at her, wide-eyed. "Even after all she said to you?"

"She might have been lying," Esofi reminded Mireille. "Just because I dislike the way Lexandrie spoke to me does not mean I think her suspicions are baseless."

"I do not believe the crown princess is lying to you," murmured Mireille, but she looked down at her hands. Then she gave Lisette a nudge. "What do you think?"

Lisette made a noncommittal noise. When Mireille nudged her again, she offered, "Lexandrie is jealous. Nobody is sitting through three-quarters of a service for her."

Mireille giggled. "Quite right! She may have had plenty of suitors back home, but now everyone's attention is on you, Princess. I don't think she likes it."

"Maybe so," said Esofi, looking down at her skirts. "Lisette, I would like you to find out more of Adale's history with Theodoar of Leikr. She claims they are not in a romantic relationship, but I know we must be realistic. If they..." Esofi's voice trailed off as she found herself unable to complete the sentence. "Well. I trust your skills. Report back to me when you have discovered anything of interest. And if you find out anything about the twins, perhaps that will aid us as well."

Lisette gave a sharp nod and hurried off, clearly glad to be excused. That left only Mireille with Esofi, which seemed to suit the baron's daughter just fine.

"Then what shall we do today, if we are not visiting the hospital?" asked Mireille.

"We are going to walk," said Esofi. "And perhaps, if we are fortunate, we shall encounter the crown princess's cousins somewhere along the way."

Chapter Four

ADALE

The twins, Brandt and Svana, had been born in the year between Albion and Adale. One might have assumed that the four would be close companions, but this was untrue. Adale and Albion had never liked spending time with the twins, and the twins seemed equally unhappy whenever circumstances forced the four together.

Brandt and Svana seemed to immediately dislike almost everyone they'd ever encountered, though they made an exception for one another. They were similar in many ways: both of medium height and oval-faced, with oddly light chestnut hair and blue eyes, quick to shout at servants and sneer at courtiers. Their one virtue was that they seemed to dislike life at court and spent most of their time at home.

Adale was in a terrible mood by the time she arrived in the throne room. She hadn't wanted to leave Esofi to begin with, and now it seemed that the twins intended to call their engagement into question. And yes, perhaps Adale was still not entirely clear on what she actually wanted, but she knew she did *not* want her cousins anywhere near Esofi.

Besides, I still have the upper hand, Adale reminded herself. *I am still the crown princess. Even if Esofi were to pick one of them over me, I am the only one who can make her a queen.*

That, of course, was working under the optimistic assumption that Esofi would not simply assign her waiting lady to murder Adale in order to clear the way to the throne. But Adale was...fairly certain that Esofi would never do such a thing.

What Adale really had to worry about was the waiting lady deciding to murder her of her own initiative.

"Adale," said her father as she entered the throne room. "There you are. You missed the arrival." He glanced at the four figures standing before him: Adale's aunt and uncle and their son and daughter. Adale plastered a bright smile across her face. Though she had no love for her cousins, her aunt and uncle were far more tolerable.

"Uncle Radulfr," she said. "I had no idea you were coming to visit. If only I'd been told to expect you."

"This was an unexpected excursion, I assure you," said Radulfr, glancing down at his children with a hint of disapproval. Neither of them even bothered to pretend to smile at Adale.

Aunt Theu was the first one to move, wrapping Adale in one of her large, stifling hugs. "You are looking so well, Adale!" she gushed. "It seems every time I come to court, you are off with your companions. I feel as though I've not seen you in years."

That was a bit of an exaggeration, for they had all seen each other at Albion's funeral three months ago, but Adale did not contradict her.

"Well, I suppose we should come directly to the heart of the matter," said Radulfr. "We have received word that Princess Esofi of Rhodia has refused to sign a marriage contract."

"She has refused nothing," said Adale quickly. Too quickly, she realized. "We've merely had some scheduling conflicts."

"The point remains," said Brandt. "She is without a fiancée."

"Only until the contract is signed," Adale insisted.

"And when will that be?" asked Svana, her tone mocking.

"Do you mean to court her then? Both of you?" demanded Adale, looking from one twin to the other. "If you've come all the way here for that, you're wasting your time. She intends to become the queen of Ieflaria, and neither of you can give her that."

"Perhaps," said Svana, snapping open a fan and fluttering it. "Perhaps not."

"There is no perhaps about it." Adale could feel her face heating. "I am the crown princess."

"And everyone knows how seriously you take your post," retorted Svana.

"I must admit, I am surprised by your hostility," added Brandt before Adale could respond. "We thought you'd be pleased to hand your responsibilities over to one of us. Or perhaps you are only being contrary to spite us."

"Brandt," said Radulfr sharply. "Mind your words."

"We do not intend to steal anything or anyone away from the crown princess." Svana addressed Adale's parents. "We only wish to offer ourselves as alternatives. Either of us would be a more suitable spouse and regent."

Adale's parents exchanged looks, and she wondered if they would tell the twins to return home. But instead, Saski said, "We understand your concerns. But Princess Esofi has already agreed to an engagement with Adale. We do not intend to stray from this plan unless we have no alternatives."

"But what if we do not?" Radulfr's voice was soft, his eyes concerned. "Intentionally or not, Adale has dealt

Princess Esofi a grave insult. We cannot be certain that Esofi means to sign a marriage contract, regardless of what she promises. I do not wish to seem as though I am seeking to seize power through my children—"

"I would not believe that you are," said Dietrich.

Radulfr's eyes shone with relief. "We cannot go on like this. We all know it. The dragons are growing more aggressive. Valenleht is filled with refugees from the surrounding coastline. If Princess Esofi can bring Talcia's magic back to Ieflaria..." He looked at Adale. "Under normal circumstances, I would never recommend passing over a rightful heir. But if Esofi will agree to marry one of the twins, at least Ieflaria will not be forced to go without her magic."

"But, wait," protested Adale. "She hasn't refused to marry me—that's just speculation. She was ill that night. It wasn't—"

"Then you've nothing to worry about, now do you?" interrupted Svana.

"This is ridiculous!" cried Adale. "Father. Mother. You cannot possibly—"

"Adale," said King Dietrich heavily. "Your uncle is correct. We cannot afford to lose Princess Esofi. If she agrees to sign the marriage contract as it is now, then we will say nothing more about it. But if she refuses..."

"I do not believe she will," Adale insisted. Both of the twins gave identical little laughs, and she turned on them. "Did you have something to contribute?"

"Nothing whatsoever," said Svana in a light, airy voice.

If only they hadn't been in the throne room, under the eyes of their parents and all the castle guards, Adale would have fought them both, simultaneously, if not simply for the joy of biting at flesh and tearing at hair. But Adale somehow managed to retain her composure.

"Very well," she said. "If that is all?"

Her father gave a nod, and Adale did not wait to be formally dismissed. She was gone from the room in an instant. Minutes later, she found herself walking the familiar path back to her room.

She would need help, that much was certain. She knew her cousins would not wait to hear Esofi's opinion on the marriage contract before they began courting her. And if the twins planned to formally court Esofi, that meant Adale would need to do the same. That meant gifts, flowers, and sweets and... Adale wasn't certain what else. She wasn't really one for formal courtship. Perhaps one of her mother's ladies could tell her the specifics. She knew it required gifts, though. And there might have been something about handkerchiefs involved.

Her mother's ladies would know. She would ask them immediately.

Adale raised a hand to her hair. Perhaps her appearance could do with some improvement too. Adale did not really think there was anything wrong with the way she looked, but compared to her cousins...

Adale forced herself to return to reality. She'd been acting as though she meant to marry Esofi and become the queen of Ieflaria. But she still wasn't certain that was what she wanted.

She was running out of time. Sooner or later, she would have to choose.

Adale thought once again of giving up her place in the succession and running off to start a new life. But for some reason, instead of relief, all she felt was a heavy sense of shame.

Her train of thought was interrupted by the sight of a man and a woman who were pressed against the wall, lips locked together in a kiss. She immediately recognized the man as one of the castle footmen—Audo, his name was. But the woman was unfamiliar. From her dress, Adale would have guessed that she was one of the royal huntsman's assistants, but Adale knew all of the huntsman's staff by name.

At the sound of Adale's incredulous half laugh, the woman pulled away from the man and ran off down the hall. Adale looked at Audo, who was still pressed against the wall, looking dazed.

"I don't even know who she was!" he protested when Adale raised her eyebrows.

Adale gave a snort and continued on her way, her mind already back to Esofi. In Adale's experience, people like Esofi were almost unattainable when one considered the amount of trouble one must go to in order to win them. Who would want to spend their energies at such a task when there were plenty of others, men and women alike, who did not need nearly as much effort in order to be persuaded?

And yet, Adale was looking forward to bringing her flowers. When had that happened? How had it happened?

Am I just being selfish? Selfish behavior was not unusual for her, but according to her parents' philosophy, giving up her freedom to marry Esofi was the height of selflessness. But Adale was less convinced. What if she had merely traded one fixation for another?

No. It is not the same. I wanted to run away so I could be happy. I want to marry Esofi so she can be happy or at least happier than she'd be with the twins. It will make me happy too, but that's not the reason I'm doing it...

...is it?

Adale glanced up and realized she was not standing in front of her own bedroom door, as she'd intended, but in front of Albion's. Her breath caught in her throat at the realization.

Adale rested her hand against the familiar wooden door. If she pretended, she could make herself believe that he was in there, just waiting for her to knock, and then he'd let her in and she'd explain everything and he'd laugh at the funny parts and get serious about the parts that were serious, but then when she was done explaining, he'd smile warmly and say that there was no need to worry because he knew exactly what to do and what to say and...

She tried the door. It was locked, and for some reason, that made her want to cry. She crouched down and tried to peer into the keyhole.

"It should have been me," she whispered into the lock. "Nobody would have missed me."

There were things, Adale knew, that people said at every funeral about the deceased. Even if the man in the casket was a drunkard who'd never worked a day in his life, upon his death, he would become the noblest soul in the entire kingdom, cruelly ripped away from his family and friends at such a young age. "Such a kind man!" they would all say to each other. "Kinder than any I'd ever met. Have you ever known such a gentle heart? And so wise, for someone so young. He was the best of his parents' children. He would have been a great man, if only, if only..."

They were the lies that had been told at every funeral since the beginning of time.

But they had not been lies when they'd said them about Albion.

"Crown Princess?" A servant—Odila, Adale's memory supplied—was eyeing her nervously. "Do you require help?"

Adale rose quickly. There was already a cramp in her knee from her unnatural position in front of the door.

"No, no, I'm all right," Adale lied, swiping at her own eyes, which had apparently become irritated by some dust.

"If there is something you require, Mistress Abbing has all the keys," said Odila. Then she scurried off, as though suddenly remembering an urgent task. Adale wanted to call a thank-you after her, but her throat felt oddly harsh. She took a few deep breaths to steady herself.

"Crown Princess?"

Adale turned around at the familiar voice. Esofi was standing there before her, attended by only one of her ladies.

"Princess," said Adale. "I thought you were going to the hospital."

"There has been a change in plans," said Esofi in a tight little voice. "Are you...are you well? Have you been locked out of your rooms?"

"What? I..." Adale looked at the door. "Oh. No. No, no. This isn't my room. It's...it is, or it was...Albion's."

"I see," said Esofi quietly.

"I don't actually know why I'm here." Adale shook her head. She wondered what Esofi, who seemed to have so much trust in the gods, would say about Albion's death. She wondered if she should ask, if it would make her feel better or worse. If Esofi said that it was all a part of some incomprehensible plan, Adale might actually slap her.

And what if she blames me for his death? There was a chance Esofi had heard the story and already did, but perhaps she'd managed to miss it. Adale knew her parents blamed her, no matter what they claimed, and always would. It was strange to realize it, but Adale did not want forgiveness. She did not, and would never, deserve it.

Esofi pressed her lips together, but she didn't seem angry. She looked...thoughtful.

"I still have those letters," she said. "The ones Albion sent me."

"Oh," said Adale. "I— Yes, I remember. You told me..."

"If you would like to review them with me," said Esofi, "I would... I think perhaps...it would be..."

"Yes," Adale interjected. "Yes, I would like that."

"Come with me, then," said Esofi.

They walked together to Esofi's rooms with Esofi's lady trailing behind them. Adale wondered where the other two had gotten to. Perhaps they were already in Esofi's room, waiting for their princess to return.

They arrived at Esofi's door, and she unlocked it. Adale had only caught a glimpse of the inside once, on the night she'd brought the kitten, but now she went inside for the first time. It was not too different from her own rooms in layout, though it did seem to be more traditionally decorated.

"Wait here," Esofi told Adale and then vanished through the door that Adale supposed led to her private rooms. Esofi's waiting lady sat down on the sofa and smiled brightly.

"What was your name, again?" Adale asked.

"Mireille of Aelora, Your Highness," said the girl. Then she leaned in a bit closer to whisper to Adale. "She likes you, you know."

"Oh," said Adale, taken aback. "Does she?"

Mireille nodded knowledgeably but said no more.

"Where is Lexandrie?" asked Esofi, returning with a bundle of old papers in her hands. The kitten was balanced on her shoulder, looking around at everything with bright gray eyes as though trying to decide where to spring to first.

"Not here, I think," said Mireille, not sounding too concerned. She found a sewing bag on the floor and plucked a half-completed embroidery piece from it. "Maybe she's trying to get some Ieflarians to fight over her glove."

Adale had no idea what this meant, and neither Mireille nor Esofi chose to elaborate. Esofi settled on the opposite couch, her skirts fluffing up around her like a great wave, and began sorting through the letters.

"I've all but the earliest ones," murmured Esofi, more to herself than Adale. "Sit beside me. They're all in Ieflarian, so you won't have any trouble reading them."

Adale took the seat next to Esofi. The princess's elaborate dress kept her from getting as close as she would have liked, but it was still closer than they'd have been allowed if they were in public. Adale glanced at Mireille, but the waiting lady seemed focused only on her embroidery, though she appeared to be having difficulty keeping down a smile.

"Here's one where he wrote of you," said Esofi, passing a sheet of paper over to Adale. "You see? He says you two went riding together."

Adale checked the date on the letter and saw that it was almost five years old. She did not remember the day or the ride, but there had been so many like it that she supposed remembering one specific trip would be impossible.

"I really must organize these," sighed Esofi. "I was reading them on the journey and now they're all out of order."

"Give me another," said Adale, suddenly feeling as though she was starving. "Any one, it doesn't matter, I don't have to be in it."

Esofi gave her another piece of paper, and Adale read every word, though most of it didn't make as much sense as she'd imagined it would, as it all responded to a conversation that Adale had never seen. But it was still a wonderful gift, proof that Albion had once been real and alive and loved...

Dearest Esofi, all the letters began. His handwriting had always been so much better than hers. Adale wondered how Esofi's letters back to him had been addressed. *Dearest Albion*, maybe? Or perhaps more formally than that, knowing Esofi...

Esofi had gone silent. She was staring at another letter and blinking very quickly, over and over and over again.

"Mireille," said Esofi at last, her voice oddly shaky. "Water, if you would..."

Mireille was up immediately, hurrying all around the suite to find a pitcher for her princess. But it seemed there was nothing to be found.

"Ridiculous!" cried Mireille. "Do they wish you to die of dehydration? Give me just a moment, Princess. I'll find you something..." And she left the suite.

Adale felt a little jolt of surprise as the door clicked shut behind her. She and Esofi were alone. Surely, Esofi felt that it was inappropriate...or perhaps her thoughts were on other things.

Esofi removed the kitten from her shoulder and set it down in her lap.

"Do you like him?" Adale asked. When Esofi looked at her in confusion, she added, "The kitten, I mean. I...probably shouldn't have given you a live animal without asking. I...I'm not very... I'm sorry."

"I do like him," said Esofi, one delicate gloved hand stroking the kitten's back, which arched under her touch. "We've decided to call him Cream." She set the pages down and looked at Adale. "Besides, I think a little bit of spontaneity won't hurt me."

"Oh," said Adale. For some reason, she was having trouble coming up with a suitable response. Esofi was so close, and they were alone, finally... Should she do something? Was Esofi expecting her to do something? Had she and Mireille planned for them to be alone? Or...maybe not. Maybe Esofi was frightened and uncomfortable and afraid Adale might try something inappropriate.

She'll beat you even more easily than she beat Theodoar. Realistically, she was in more danger from Esofi than Esofi was from her.

"Your cousins mean to court me," said Esofi. It was not a question.

"Yes," said Adale. "Who told you?"

Esofi shrugged. "I guessed. You already told me they would be suitable candidates. It seems they've had the same idea."

"Yes, but I've changed my mind," said Adale. "I mean to marry you."

"So you say," murmured Esofi, gazing up at Adale through her eyelashes. Adale very slowly brought one hand up to cup the side of Esofi's face, half expecting the princess to scream or slap her.

"Mind the powder," said Esofi very quietly. "You'll have white hands."

"I don't mind," Adale replied, suddenly feeling as though she was in a dream. She brushed her thumb across Esofi's lips, the gesture leaving a little spot of pink color on her fingertip. Esofi closed her eyes.

"Shall I stop?" whispered Adale.

"No," breathed Esofi.

Adale leaned forward and pressed her lips to Esofi's. Everything about her was soft, as if the princess was made of nothing but feathers and cream. She was warm, too, and Adale wanted to pull her close, to press their bodies together. But perhaps that would have been pushing her luck a bit too far, and besides, the complicated and alien Rhodian dress left her uncertain.

"Crown Princess," murmured Esofi against Adale's mouth. She was not returning the kiss, but she wasn't resisting, either. It occurred to Adale that the princess had no idea what she was meant to do in this situation.

Adale broke the kiss, and Esofi opened her eyes. Most of her lip paint was gone, but she didn't seem to have noticed.

"I-I'm sorry," said Adale awkwardly. "I..."

"Do not be," said Esofi. "If I'd wanted you to stop, I would have said so." She took Adale's hand and laced their fingers together. "Or do you regret it already?"

"No!" cried Adale. "Not at all. Not like that."

"Good." Esofi gave a small nod. Adale couldn't see her moving, but Esofi seemed to somehow be sitting nearer to her than she'd been just a few minutes before. Esofi's other hand moved to touch the side of Adale's face. The texture of her lace glove felt odd against her cheek.

"You never wear powder," observed Esofi.

"No," said Adale. "I've never liked it."

"Mm," said Esofi. "Perhaps you're wiser than I. The trouble is, once you begin wearing it, you can never stop, or people will think you're ill."

Adale laughed, and Esofi withdrew her hand. "But then you must not have any trouble pretending to be sick when you want to get out of something."

"Get out of something?" Esofi repeated.

"You know. Ceremonies. Or services."

Esofi blinked up at her. "Oh. I suppose I never thought of that." But fortunately, she didn't seem offended or annoyed by the implication that she might want to shirk her responsibilities. "I suppose anything I would have wanted to avoid involved my siblings, back in Rhodia."

"You have many siblings, don't you?" asked Adale. She couldn't recall where she'd heard that, but it sounded correct to her ears.

"Yes," said Esofi. "Two brothers, three sisters."

"And you weren't close to any of them?"

"No. I suppose I wasn't." Esofi looked distant. "I always knew...we all knew...that I would be leaving someday. We never discussed it, but I think we all decided it would be easier for everyone if I just..."

"That's not right." Adale was suddenly angry on Esofi's behalf. "You didn't deserve that, you should have been—they should have done the opposite, if they knew they were going to lose you!"

"Perhaps," said Esofi.

"What about your parents?" asked Adale.

Esofi swallowed visibly. "My father is a good man," she said at last. "Our people love him for his patience and understanding."

"And your mother?"

"Oh, they love her too," said Esofi in a brittle tone. "Everyone loves her."

"I am sorry," whispered Adale.

Esofi seemed to brighten a little. "Never mind that—I am free of them now. Ieflaria will be my home from now on. I will have another family, a better one." Her fingers tightened around Adale's.

"A family," repeated Adale. "Do you mean...?"

"What?" asked Esofi.

"Everyone is wondering about heirs," Adale said. "I suppose...there is the Change." The Change was a ritual performed by the priestesses of Dayluue. Most people tried it at least once in their life just for the novelty, though it wouldn't last for very long unless the person being transformed had a soul that was willing to remain in its new body forever.

Adale knew her own soul was not willing, but a few hours would probably be enough time. Other women had managed it.

"Ah," said Esofi. She suddenly seemed nervous. "I did not think you were ready to speak of such things."

"Maybe I'm not," admitted Adale. "Maybe I won't be for a few years yet."

"We have time." Esofi looked distinctly relieved, and Adale wondered if she was dreading the possibility of children just as much as Adale was. "When you are ready..."

"And if I'm never ready?" Adale regretted the words as soon as she'd spoken them, even though they were, as far as Adale knew, the truth.

"Then we never will," said Esofi. "There will be other heirs, other families. Your line will not die out with us. I'm sure the older nobles and your parents' advisors won't like it, but they cannot force us."

"You are truly certain you will not become impatient with me?" asked Adale.

"I swear it before Iolar and Talcia and any other gods who may be listening," said Esofi firmly. She still had not released her hold on Adale's hand. "I am in no more of a hurry than you are."

"Oh," said Adale. "I thought perhaps...some noblewomen want nothing more than to start producing heirs."

"Not I," said Esofi. "There are so many other things to accomplish, after all. We've no shortage of children in the world. What we do have a shortage of is battlemages." Esofi looked guilty. "Perhaps I should have gone to the temple today."

"Why didn't you?" asked Adale.

Esofi glanced down at the kitten in her lap. "Selfishness, I suppose."

"How do you mean?"

"I was curious about your cousins," Esofi admitted. "I'd hoped to encounter them today to see for myself what they were like, but they retired to their rooms so quickly, I could not even catch a glimpse. I know I should be focusing on the establishment of the university, but I've been spending so much time on it, I thought a single day away wouldn't harm anyone."

"And has it?" asked Adale.

"Perhaps. Perhaps not." Esofi gave a little shrug. "Still, I shouldn't be indulging myself so. Ieflarians die every time a dragon attacks. I should—"

"I don't think one day will make a difference when the university hasn't even been built yet," pointed out Adale.

"We cannot know," Esofi said. "And now I find myself wondering if we should begin classes without the building. Construction will take a year, at the very least. But if we can begin training people earlier...it might make a difference."

"Well, the day is not done yet," Adale said. "Perhaps you can still go. Skip the hospital and go straight to the Temple of Talcia. They'll be delighted to see you, I'm sure. And I can...I can accompany you if you like."

"Yes," said Esofi, her fingertips playing across the surface of Adale's palm. "I—only if you want to, though. I know you are...not so comfortable in temples."

"It's not the temples as much as the services," admitted Adale. "But nevertheless, I will go with you gladly. I want to be where you are. Wherever that is."

Esofi reached out and touched Adale's face again, her open palm resting against Adale's cheek. Adale leaned in, wrapped an arm around Esofi, and pulled her close enough to press their foreheads together. Esofi's lips were irresistibly close, and Adale kissed her again. This time, Esofi returned the kiss, though she still seemed a bit uncertain.

Adale broke the kiss for a moment so that she could kiss Esofi's nose instead, which earned her an adorable little giggle. All the anxiety seemed to have left Esofi's body, and the princess curled closer to her, so close that Adale could feel Esofi's heartbeat, slow and rhythmic, against her chest.

"You're so beautiful," marveled Adale.

"You truly think so?" There was genuine doubt in Esofi's voice.

"I do," said Adale, trailing one hand down Esofi's back. "But surely you hear that all the time?"

There was the sound of someone fiddling with the lock outside, and Esofi immediately straightened up. The two disentangled rapidly, returning to their original sitting positions within a matter of seconds. A minute later, the door opened, and in came Mireille balancing a tray with a pitcher of water in one hand.

"Here I am!" she cried cheerfully. "So sorry for the delay. I wasn't too long, was I?"

If Mireille could see the damage that Adale had done to Esofi's makeup, she said nothing about it as she set the tray down on the nearest surface and began to pour out goblets of water.

"Here," said Esofi, picking up another one of Albion's letters. Adale had almost forgotten about them. "This one mentions you as well, I think. I'll be surprised if we don't find half of them have your name in them somewhere..."

Adale looked down at the letter but found that she could not focus on the words while Esofi's body was so near to hers, close enough that Adale could feel the princess's slow, measured breathing and see the gentle rise and fall of her chest. She wanted...

Adale forced her attention back to the page in front of her. But it seemed that she was not the only one having difficulty focusing.

"Mireille," said Esofi after a few painfully long minutes. "I think I would like to visit the Temple of Talcia today."

"Oh," said Mireille, the disappointment in her tone evident. "Shall I find Lady Lexandrie, then?"

"Oh, never mind her," said Esofi dismissively. "The crown princess will accompany us as well, I think...?" Esofi glanced at Adale.

"Yes!" said Adale quickly. "Yes, of course, I...yes."

Mireille's look of dismay had been replaced by a wide grin.

"Good," said Esofi, setting her kitten down on the floor before rising to her feet. "Give me fifteen minutes to prepare, and I shall meet you at the stables. Mireille, tell the hostlers to ready a carriage."

"Never mind that, I'll do it myself," said Adale.

"You?" asked Esofi. "But that would not be proper."

"No, really, it's fine," said Adale, getting up as well. "You need your lady, and I've nothing to do in the meantime."

Adale left the room with a warm feeling in her chest and a spring in her step. She wondered if Daphene or Lethea were sober enough to accompany her on the trip, but then she wondered if she wanted them with her, propriety be damned. Esofi's lady would be there, and that was technically enough, but...

If only Theodoar was still here, she knew he could behave for long stretches of time if she bribed him enough.

Adale burst into her rooms, hands shaking from a strange mixture of anxiety and joy. "Are either of you awake?" she called, banging her fist on the door that led to the accompanying rooms. "Daphene! Lethea!"

It was Daphene that fumbled her way to the door, eyes still closed and hair in disarray. She might have been wearing last night's dress.

"Castle on fire?" she mumbled.

"No, I—"

"Don't care." And she went to close the door in Adale's face. Adale jammed her boot in the way before it could close.

"I need an attendant," said Adale. "How quickly can you be ready? We are going to the Temple of Talcia."

"In the middle of the night?" murmured Daphene, rubbing her sleeve against her eyes. "Why?"

"It's almost noon," said Adale sharply. "I need you to come and distract Esofi's waiting lady for me."

"Esofi?" Daphene seemed to wake a little. "Is that what this is about?"

"Yes," said Adale. "I need you to meet me down at the stables in fifteen minutes."

"*Fift*—!" But Adale was gone before Daphene could even begin her complaint.

The stables were not too crowded this time of day, though the hostler put on quite a show of being very busy the moment Adale walked through the doors. Adale told them of Esofi's plans and then left them to prepare the carriage. In the meantime, she visited Warcry, who was in his stall.

"I've nothing for you today," said Adale as he nipped at her collar, clearly hoping for apples or boiled sweets. Adale's gaze went to the still-empty stall beside him. There was a slightly discolored spot on the door where the nameplate had been removed.

"I'm sorry," Adale said quietly, rubbing her palm against Warcry's nose. "I'm sorry." She pressed her face into his neck and inhaled his familiar horse scent, warm hair and dry straw. At least he didn't blame her. He might, if he were capable. But he wasn't, so he didn't.

Esofi and Mireille arrived shortly, followed by Daphene ten minutes later. They got in the carriage and, accompanied by more guards than Adale thought was remotely necessary, headed out to the Temple of Talcia.

"Where are you going to get your students from?" asked Adale, trying to strike up another conversation. "Most of our citizens with Talcia's magic just ignore it their whole lives."

"I know," said Esofi. "But I'm hoping an impressive new university will encourage them to start thinking about appreciating their gifts. Besides, after they complete their education, they will be all but assured a prestigious job defending their country."

"If they are courageous enough," pointed out Adale. "Some might be less eager to fight a dragon."

"Perhaps," said Esofi. "But for the sake of protecting their homes..."

"You must think I'm useless." Adale laughed. "I've never even seen a live dragon, except from a very great distance, and it might have just been a very large hawk."

"I would not want you to seek one out if you've no means of defending yourself!" cried Esofi. "Besides..."

"Besides what?" asked Adale, for Esofi suddenly looked very worried.

"Besides, I think you may see one soon enough," Esofi murmured.

"What do you mean?" asked Adale.

"They are moving inward," said Esofi. "Even your generals have spotted the patterns in their attacks. I believe their true target is Birsgen."

"But we've been beating them!" protested Adale. "Most of the time, at least. And besides, we have your battlemages now. And you."

Esofi's severe expression lightened for just a moment. "Perhaps you are right. Even if an attack does come, maybe we will be able to fight them off with minimal losses. Still, it is never an easy victory when one fights a dragon."

"Not even for you?" asked Adale.

"No," said Esofi. "Not even for me. Every dragon has a unique personality and fighting style. It is much like fighting a Man, I suppose. And they are clever, even if they've lost most of their gifts. I consider myself very fortunate that I've never been forced to face one alone."

"I think you could do it," said Adale. "If you had to."

Esofi gave a small laugh. "I pray it never comes to that."

The carriage came to a halt, and they disembarked at the steps of the Temple of Talcia. It was nowhere near as large and impressive as the Great Temple of Iolar, though still, Adale thought, perfectly acceptable.

Esofi, though, was frowning deeply as she walked up the black marble steps that led to the temple itself. It was similar in layout to the Temple of Iolar, with a walled courtyard in front of the temple proper. This courtyard, however, was not quite as well-kept, and it seemed that many of the flowers had become overgrown.

The courtyard wasn't busy at all. Aside from the temple birds, a staple of any of Talcia's temples, the only signs of life there were a pair of acolytes, who were working to refill the feeders with seeds. At the sight of the princess's approach, they began whispering to each other.

"I wish to speak to the archpriestess," announced Esofi. "I have important news for her."

The archpriestess was an old woman with a soft and wrinkled face and long, silver hair. She leaned heavily on a polished black walking stick for support as she emerged from the temple. An ordinary-ranked priestess was just behind her, looking concerned. Both women were dressed in the traditional midnight-blue colors of the goddess.

Esofi hurried forward, pausing only to curtsy briefly, before beginning to speak animatedly to the holy women. Adale glanced over at Daphene. Despite being dressed and upright, she still seemed to be asleep. Mireille was bright and awake, but her eyes had a sort of glazed look to them as well.

She'd forgotten how uncomfortable she always felt in temples. Even before Albion's death, she'd never quite felt as though she belonged in them. Now, it felt like the entire temple had been constructed specifically to mock her.

Glancing around, Adale felt that familiar old resentment rising up in her chest. Foolish. It was all foolish. If the gods were still watching, if they hadn't wandered off to do whatever the gods did before they'd created mankind, they were probably laughing at the antics of their children.

But... Adale hesitated. It had not been so when she'd spoken to Esofi about the Temple of Adranus. She had meant what she said, that she believed the gods wanted mankind to think and understand. Or at least, she'd meant it at the time. When she was next to Esofi, she could believe that maybe the gods were something other than malicious and mocking.

But when she was standing in a temple, with its cold stone walls and blatantly materialistic displays, it was hard to believe that she had ever felt anything other than disdain.

The archpriestess was now indicating something off in another direction, probably telling Esofi about the size of the temple's lands. Adale knew she should be listening, but it was hard enough to keep her breathing from coming in jagged, heavy spurts without having to think about Esofi's hypothetical university.

The University of Esofi. Adale gave a short, awkward sound that was less of a laugh and more of a sharp exhale. Fortunately, Esofi and the priestesses did not seem to notice.

Adale had the sudden need to move, to run. She began to walk the length of the courtyard, leaving the two waiting ladies to stare after her in confusion. Carved into the courtyard's inner walls were scenes of forests under moonlight, complete with wolves and deer and rabbits. There was something odd in the marble clouds, too. Adale paused to give it a hard stare and realized that it was a dragon.

Adale found it strange that such a violent and destructive creature would be depicted in any temple. Perhaps Esofi would have an explanation, if Adale asked.

The priestesses were leading Esofi in the direction of the inner temple, where services would be held, and Adale hurried after them. The archpriestess was saying something about the size of their congregations, and Esofi was nodding with rapt interest.

Inside the temple was not unlike any other temple, dimly lit and silent and a little bit musty. Adale had been inside this temple many times before for Talcia's holy days, and it looked more or less unchanged. Perhaps the priestesses had rearranged some statues or furniture out of boredom, or perhaps Adale's memory was simply failing her.

"Our temple seats approximately one thousand," the archpriestess was saying. "Though we only fill that many spots on the holy days, and then of course, we are terribly overcrowded. Do you attend the lunar services?"

"Always," said Esofi lightly. Lunar services were not quite holy days, but they weren't quite ordinary either. Unlike Iolar's sunrise and sunset services, which were held once a week, the lunar service took place only once a month on the night of the full moon. Adale had not attended one since childhood.

"Then perhaps our numbers will increase," said the archpriestess. Adale had a feeling she was right. Once people found out that the princess was a regular visitor to the temple, they would flood in simply to be seen in the same location.

"How many of Talcia's temples are there in Birsgen?" asked Esofi.

"Four, including this one," the archpriestess said.

"A small number, for such a large city," murmured Esofi. "And you take in students for the study of magic?"

"When they come to us." The archpriestess gave a shrug. "We've had none this year, and most of the ones we've had in the past turn out to have Adranus's gifts instead. Even the girls. It is a pity, but we've come to accept it."

Esofi went quiet, apparently deep in thought.

"It will have to do for now," she said at last. "I am confident that things will change soon enough, though. If the building of the new university gets her attention..."

"It will still be a decade before any new mages are old enough to come to us for training." The archpriestess's eyes were hard, unimpressed. "Maybe longer."

"Better a decade than never," Esofi replied calmly. "And, once news of the university spreads, perhaps we will find some of our magically inclined citizens reconsidering their neglect of the gift."

The archpriestess said nothing, and Adale thought she understood how the old woman felt. After what had to be decades of silence and inattention, mustering up even the smallest spark of hope probably felt like a waste of effort, doomed to end in nothing more than disappointment.

"Some of the mages I've brought with me from Rhodia are trained as teachers," Esofi continued. "They are prepared to serve under your supervision and educate our new students. I have already approved their curriculum, but perhaps you would like to review it as well."

The archpriestess gave a small nod but said nothing more. Esofi made a quiet humming noise to herself and began to move quietly through the temple, exploring. Adale noticed that even though the archpriestess seemed unmoved, the other priestesses were whispering eagerly to each other.

Fortunately, the visit did not drag on for as long as Adale had feared it might. Soon enough, they were back in the courtyard and descending the steps to the street. Esofi was quieter than Adale would have expected—she'd thought Esofi would be chattering animatedly about all her plans and hopes for the future, but this was not the case.

"In Rhodia," she said at last, "the ceiling of the Temple of Talcia is made of glass. They uncover it for the lunar services, and it's indescribably lovely. I think I would like to do something similar here."

"Oh," said Adale, but she supposed it was still better than burning it to the ground.

When they arrived back at the castle, it was past lunchtime, but Adale told Esofi not to worry about that and asked her to meet her in the courtyard at the same place they'd taken tea with Queen Saski. Esofi agreed, and Adale set off to the kitchens to see what leftovers she could find for them.

When Adale went out to the gardens, she saw that Esofi and Mireille were sitting at the table, as planned.

But, to her horror, Svana and Brandt were there as well, sitting in chairs on either side of the princess. Svana was holding flowers, and Brandt had a small silk box.

Adale cleared her throat and set the "borrowed" dishes down on the table. Esofi smiled brightly at her.

"Oh, there you are," she said. "I've finally met your cousins!"

"I see," said Adale unhappily. "Brandt, what do you have there?"

"Just a simple gift to welcome Princess Esofi to our nation," he said, smiling wide enough to show teeth. "We were so disappointed when we learned she had already gone out for the day."

"I imagine you were," said Adale. "Well, as we missed the noontime meal, I—"

"Oh, do not banish us so quickly, cousin." Svana was now threading flowers from the bouquet into Esofi's hair. To Adale's horror, Esofi did not appear to be irritated by it, but was smiling as brightly as ever. "We've not been to court in so long. Tell us how you've been occupying yourself."

Adale grabbed a tiny sandwich off the dish and gestured to some servants, signaling them to bring drinks.

"There is little to tell," she began. "I—"

"As we suspected," sighed Brandt.

"Princess Esofi," said Svana, apparently forgetting that she'd only a moment ago asked Adale a question. "I have heard that you play the violin."

Adale was about to object—she had never heard such a thing, and she was the one who actually lived in the castle!—but Esofi nodded vigorously around her mouthful of food.

"I should like to hear you play someday, then," said Svana. "And perhaps I can sing for you in return."

Adale's blood flashed hot at the suggestion. For all her cousin's faults, she could not criticize Svana's unspeakably and infuriatingly beautiful voice. Valenleht was a port city, and Svana had been trained by the Mer. If there was any woman on the continent with the power to make others fall in love with her with her voice alone, Svana was that woman.

But she kissed me. Twice.

"I would like that, I think." Esofi was smiling serenely. "I only wonder where my violin is. The servants put all my belongings in such odd places after I arrived. My ladies are still finding my stockings."

"Oh, these servants." Brandt rolled his eyes. "Useless, the lot of them. Now, at our estate, we have a fine staff that has served our family loyally for generations. If you saw the difference, you would flee Birsgen in horror."

"Here, you!" cried Svana to the nearest servant in a high, sharp voice, as though she was commanding a dog. "Bring my mandolin." She smiled at Esofi. "It's such a lovely day. I'll play something for you, and then you can do the same."

"Oh." Esofi was beginning to look a bit overwhelmed. "Adale, do you play?"

"No," admitted Adale. "I had lessons on the pianoforte when I was young, but nothing ever came of it."

"Crown Princess Adale is not so accomplished as one would expect for a woman of her status," said Svana gleefully. "You should see her try to dance."

"I'm sure that's not true," said Esofi.

"Oh no, it is," Brandt assured her.

"Well, I think it is unfair to expect anyone to be accomplished in all things," Esofi murmured. "After all, we all have some area in which we are lacking."

"Even you, Princess?" Svana asked. "I refuse to believe it."

Esofi laughed, a tinge of pinkness showing on her cheeks.

"On the subject of dancing," said Brandt, "Svana and I have been away from court for so long, we've missed the grand balls of Birsgen. We wish to host one in a few days' time and would be honored if you would attend, Princess Esofi."

"Oh!" said Esofi. "That does sound lovely. I've not been to any Ieflarian parties yet."

"Then I expect you will be impressed," said Svana.

"A ball, during mourning?" interjected Adale. "Don't you think that's disrespectful?"

"I don't see how it's any different than running around in the forest getting drunk and killing animals," retorted Svana sharply. "Besides, the mourning period is practically over. Don't pretend like you aren't as tired of it as the rest of us."

Adale wasn't sure what was more infuriating—Svana's disregard for Albion's death or the fact that she was completely correct in her assessment that Adale wanted to be done with it.

Biting back the worst of her rage, she merely said, "You will look ridiculous in a black ball gown. Like a widow."

"Then we shall not burden you with an invitation," Svana snapped, her hands clenching into fists. She wanted to fight just as much as Adale did, but they could not—not with Esofi looking on. Fortunately, a servant finally arrived with Svana's mandolin, and the argument was dropped.

"Here, do you know many Ieflarian songs?" asked
Svana, her fingers gliding over the strings as if by instinct,
picking out a familiar tune. "I'm afraid I don't know any
of Rhodia."

"A few..." began Esofi, but Svana was already playing.
It was a slow, melancholy tune that Adale only half
recognized, not at all the traditional love ballad she'd been
expecting. Svana began to sing, her sweet, high voice
mournful.

> *"Once upon a midnight*
> *When I was far from home*
> *I wandered through the wilds*
> *And thought myself alone*
>
> *The mountain flowers were blooming*
> *In spite of snow to be*
> *And there I saw her walking*
> *Her cloak swept o'er the leaves*
>
> *Her eyes were like the evening*
> *T'were stars beneath her skin*
> *And when her lips did touch mine*
> *I felt her light within.*
> *And now that it is winter*
> *With no work to attend*
> *Perhaps I shall go walking*
> *And meet her once again."*

Esofi was leaning forward, one elbow rested on the
table. Her eyes were soft as she listened, and Adale felt her
hatred for her cousin simmer away into something softer,
at least for a moment.

"ESOFI HAS GIVEN us her answer," said Saski.

Adale stood before her parents in their room once again. Two days had passed since the arrival of the twins, but only now had her mother and father summoned her to speak with them privately.

"Her answer?" Adale repeated. "To the betrothal? What does she say?"

Saski gave a small sigh and looked at Dietrich.

"What?" cried Adale.

"She has said that she does not wish to make her decision lightly," said Saski. "And given the circumstances, I find I cannot blame her. She says she is considering your cousins, and I could do nothing to dissuade her."

"What?" Adale could not help but feel betrayed. She had really thought Esofi had been starting to like her. They had read Albion's letters together and shared their fears of the future. Esofi had *kissed* her! What more could anyone—

"Listen to me," said Saski sharply. "She says she will announce her choice at the end of the mourning period. Your father and I will host a ball on that day, one that she cannot possibly refuse to attend. She will announce her decision there, and the contract will be signed on the spot. In the meantime, *you* will do nothing to jeopardize this."

"If you hate the twins, send them home!" cried Adale.

"I cannot, do you realize that?" asked Saski. "If she refuses to marry you, she must marry *someone*. They are the most suitable candidates."

Adale put her face in her hands. "I thought I was doing well. I really did."

To her surprise, it was Dietrich who put a comforting hand on her shoulder.

"We have noticed that you are spending time with Princess Esofi," he said. "And we appreciate the effort you are making. But you must understand: in her eyes, your romantic compatibility is only a secondary concern. Esofi has been raised to be a queen. She will choose the partner who will make the best co-regent. Regardless of her personal feelings."

"Then I don't have a chance," said Adale. She resolved to get in as many kisses as she could in the meantime, just to spite whichever of her cousins Esofi ultimately chose.

"We do not believe so," said Saski. "What your father and I see in you is far more impressive than what we see in your cousins."

"Being nice to servants isn't enough to run a country!" protested Adale.

"It is not merely kindness, Adale," said Saski. "It is their knowledge that you see them as Men, rather than slaves or cattle. What the Xytan Empire did to us has not quite faded from our collective memories. And you must realize that many of our citizens see the nobility as unapproachable and distant, despite our best efforts. Oftentimes, they are afraid to tell us their true thoughts, so greatly have they venerated us. But you have never felt compelled to hide your true self. I believe you could connect with our people in a way that no one from the Verheicht line ever has before."

"But Esofi knows so many more things," said Adale. "She knows how to—to fight dragons and plan battles. She thinks about the dangers—"

"And you think about our people," completed Saski. "You are not meant to have the same traits as Esofi, Adale. You are meant to balance her. Esofi comes from a nation that, if I may be blunt, is known for its poor opinion of commoners. She needs you beside her so she does not treat our people the way her mother treats the Rhodians."

That was not the first time Adale had heard someone imply there was something amiss with Esofi's mother. Remembering Esofi's own words on the subject, she frowned deeply. "What do we know of the queen of Rhodia?"

Saski looked surprised. "Queen Gaelle? She is—" She looked at Dietrich. "—she is nothing like Esofi to say the very least, and we can thank the gods for that. Why do you ask?"

"I only wish to understand Esofi better," said Adale. "Her upbringing must have been very different from mine."

"You can scarcely imagine," said Saski dryly.

Adale set her jaw and attempted to yawn without actually opening her mouth. Under normal circumstances, she would not have cared about being seen yawning in the middle of a service, but this was the lunar service, and Esofi was sitting only a few seats over.

Against her better judgment, Adale had accepted the help of her mother's ladies in preparing for the service, since Daphene and Lethea had an admittedly weak grasp on looking presentable for religious functions. Then, to Adale's horror, her mother had announced that they were *all* going to the service.

Now Adale sat in the front row of the Great Temple of Talcia, dressed in a gown she hadn't even known she owned until a few hours ago, with too many bracelets around her wrists and an uncomfortable silver hairpiece digging into her scalp. The ancient archpriestess seemed completely unfazed by the presence of the entire royal family in her temple, as well as the presence of all the lesser nobles, aristocrats, and upwardly mobile merchants who had followed them. She simply went on hobbling through the rituals as though this service was no different than any of the others that had preceded it.

Adale risked another glance at Esofi. The princess was watching the service attentively, a peaceful smile on her face. Occupying the seats between the princess and Adale were, of course, the twins. There was no escaping them.

Adale let her thoughts wander. Then, when she was bored of even that, she set her attention to counting the stars painted on the enormous mural of the night sky behind the altar. After what felt like an eternity, the ceremony came to a close. Unfortunately, she could not escape straightaway. The crowd was taking its time to disperse and her mother seemed to be indulging them, accepting greetings from her subjects as though she had nothing better to do.

Adale had initially planned on staying for as long as Esofi did, but the service had left her short-tempered and irritated. Fortunately, the streets were well-lit and still reasonably crowded from the service. Adale began the short walk back up to the castle, and if a pair of well-intentioned watchmen followed her from a respectful distance until they were certain she'd made it home safely, she told herself that she did not notice.

The castle was quiet still, and she was grateful for that. As she began the journey back to her room, pulling fitfully at the comb in her hair, her gaze fell upon a pair of servants who had clearly been counting on the hall being empty for a while longer, judging by the intensity of their kiss.

The couple consisted of a palace maid and a tall, dark-haired woman that Adale realized she'd already seen once before.

"You again!" said Adale. The hunter woman broke the kiss and turned to Adale with a strange smile. Taking advantage of the distraction, the maid ducked out from under the woman's arm and escaped down the hall, giggling madly.

"Here, don't you have work to do?" asked Adale, well aware of her own hypocrisy. The woman's smile only widened. Her lips were a strange, dark color, almost black. "Or are you just out to kiss everyone in the castle?"

"Not everyone, Crown Princess," said the woman. "For example, not you."

Adale frowned, moderately offended. "Well, why not?"

The woman laughed and bolted past Adale, quick as a deer. Stunned, Adale spun around in time to see the last of the woman's long black hair whip around the nearest corner. Adale hurried after her, but when she turned the corner, the woman was gone.

Chapter Five

ESOFI

The presents from the twins were already beginning to pile up, but Esofi was having difficulty focusing on them. There had been another dragon strike yesterday, at Adelsroda, a town only three days ride south of Birsgen. The refugees were already moving north under royal guard and expected to arrive in Birsgen within the week.

On Esofi's desk rested a map of Ieflaria marked in bright red ink at the site of every dragon attack in the past year. The marks left a wide but distinct inward spiral pattern, with Birsgen at the heart.

The next attack would be at the capital. She could feel it.

She wished she could set aside the entire matter of her engagement until the dragon issue was resolved. It was a struggle to even keep a level head, for she was quite unused to this degree of romantic interest. Back home, everyone had understood that she was engaged to a foreign prince and to pursue her would have been a waste of time. Even if someone had been inclined to court her, Esofi would never have accepted it. Probably.

Some days had been lonelier than others.

Her ladies were not being shy about making their opinions of her suitors known. Lexandrie was staunchly in favor of Svana, while Mireille asked her of Adale almost constantly, and Lisette seemed to prefer Brandt, citing that the question of heirs would come up sooner or later.

At long last, there was a knock at the door. Lexandrie, who had been reading quietly in her usual spot on the sofa, rose to answer it. His Majesty's young squire, Ilbert, was standing there, waiting to escort Esofi to her meeting with King Dietrich and his generals.

That day, they would be discussing the permanent placement of the battlemages until more could be trained. The call for magically gifted Ieflarians had been sent out, and Esofi could only hope, for now.

For the meeting, Esofi brought only Lexandrie with her. Esofi's annoyance with her cousin had not quite dissipated yet, but Lexandrie was acting as though nothing was wrong, and Esofi didn't have the energy to quarrel with her. Besides, Lexandrie was the only one of her ladies who would be of any sort of use during the meeting. Though her magic was not as powerful as Esofi's, she still had a good eye for details and a mind for strategy.

They departed with Ilbert taking the lead. He was a well-behaved young man or at least wise enough to pretend to be so when he was around Esofi. She wasn't sure who his parents were, but she supposed they must be important, for King Dietrich to have chosen their son to be his squire.

They met in the war room, which reminded Esofi a great deal of the one back home in Rho Dianae, where her parents and all their advisors would occasionally discuss grim things with somber faces. Esofi and her siblings had been allowed to attend these meetings under the condition that they would not make a single sound throughout.

The large table in the middle of the room was painted with a map of the entire continent, Ieflaria at the center. Gleaming silver pieces had been placed upon it to mark the recent dragon attacks, mirroring the map on her own desk.

Esofi knew the names of all the military commanders that His Majesty had invited but could not match the names to the faces. The Ieflarian military was a bit different from the Rhodian, and the pins and stripes that indicated rank were strange and unfamiliar to Esofi. Fortunately, King Dietrich arrived quickly, saving Esofi from having to hide her ignorance, and the meeting began.

"They are coming from the northeast," said Captain Lehmann, indicating the Silver Isles on the map. "Their routes are unpredictable, but they do not seem to ever travel through Xytae. They would rather pass over the sea than deal with the Xytan Legion, it seems."

"We've seen them flying overhead," confirmed a neutroi who was dressed in a naval uniform—Esofi supposed they must have been an admiral. "Unfortunately, they're too fast for our warships. We're lucky if we manage to get in a few shots of the harpoons before they're already gone. Hitting them in the wings is the only way we've managed to kill them, and that's only happened twice."

"Your Majesty, you know our borders are simply too long for us to defend it all," said one of the men. "We can afford to leave the south, because Vesolda would never march on us, but it is not so with Xytae. The battlemages must be spread across the northern and eastern borders—"

"No," said Esofi stubbornly. "They will be spread too thinly. They must remain here."

One of the women gave an exasperated sigh. "Do you intend to let them attack Birsgen, then?"

"They do not require my permission to do that," said Esofi. "It is the vaults beneath the castle that call to them—that is the reason for their movements inward." She thought of the place where her dowry was being kept. No doubt her addition made the scent even more irresistible. "We must act as though an attack on Birsgen could come at any moment."

There was a knock at the door. All fell silent and looked to it in confusion—who would interrupt such an important meeting? But the knocking only became more insistent. After a puzzled pause, King Dietrich strode over and pulled the doors open.

Standing before him was one of Archmage Eads's apprentices, red-faced and sweating. He doubled over to catch his breath.

"Your Majesty!" he sputtered. "You must come quickly!"

"What has happened?" demanded King Dietrich. "Speak, now!"

"We have had a sign from Lady Talcia!" he cried, and then went back to gasping.

Esofi grabbed her skirts and surged forward. "Where!?" she cried. The apprentice looked up at her and pointed down the hall.

"They've gathered in the healing ward," he said.

Esofi had no idea where that was, but fortunately, King Dietrich was already moving. With Lexandrie at her heels, she followed him down the halls that were becoming more familiar with every passing day and into an area of the castle that she'd never visited before. They came to a large set of doors painted with symbols of Adranus, and King Dietrich threw them open.

Gathered inside the room was a strange assortment of castle staff and Birsgeners, all looking shaken and confused, sitting wherever they could find a space. The castle healers seemed to be at a loss, running around frantically but without purpose. The chief healer, a high-ranking priest of Adranus, was arguing hotly with Archmage Eads.

"What is going on?" demanded King Dietrich, and the room fell silent—for a moment. Then one of the Birsgener women started crying loudly.

"My lord," began Archmage Eads. "We, that is, I—"

Lexandrie gave a sudden gasp, and Esofi moved closer to the weeping woman. She was dressed in the ordinary clothes of a Birsgen shopkeeper, and her head was lowered. She seemed to be holding something in her hands, something that glittered like sapphires.

It was the light of magic.

Esofi felt her heart stop for just a moment.

"You were not born with this, were you?" Esofi asked, drawing nearer. The woman's pale eyes, rimmed with redness, met her own.

"None of them were," said the priest of Adranus from behind Esofi. "When the first one came in, we thought it was merely a mistake in our recordkeeping or an oversight."

"I told you," spat one of the men who was standing, arms crossed and eyes narrowed in rage. He had the scent of a tanner about him, and Esofi found herself wishing she had an orange to cover the smell. "They thought I was wrong. As if I lived thirty-five years not knowing I had magic."

Esofi did a quick count of the room. There were eleven patients in total, but nobody could say how many new mages were scattered throughout Ieflaria, waiting to discover their gifts.

"I have never heard of anyone being granted magic later in their life," volunteered Archmage Eads. "In Ieflaria, it has always been taught that Talcia only grants magic to babies at the moment they draw their first breath."

"It is so in Rhodia as well," said Esofi, her head spinning. She'd barely begun her work in Ieflaria, and Talcia had already made her approval known. How could this be?

But Esofi realized that she could wonder about that later. At the moment, she had a room of frightened citizens to reassure. She released the woman's hands and stood.

"I'm sure I cannot imagine how you're all feeling right now," said Esofi. "But in time, I hope you will realize what a wonderful gift you've been given—the opportunity to defend your city in the coming months, rather than leave the fight to foreigners."

None of the Birsgeners looked particularly enthused.

"I have three children," said one of the other women at last. "I can't risk my life to fight dragons. You have to understand that."

Esofi bit back an impassioned speech about serving one's country, and instead said, "Even so, you must be trained. You could harm yourself or another if you lose control. We are setting up a university in the Temple District, but now it is clear we cannot wait for construction to be complete." She looked to King Dietrich for his approval, but before he could reply, the doors swung open again and Adale strode in. She paused for a moment to take in the gathered group and then gave a half-incredulous laugh.

"So it's true?" she asked.

"Adale," said King Dietrich disapprovingly. "Why are you here?"

"Why shouldn't I be?" responded Adale. "It's my country too. If we've had a sign from—from Talcia, or whoever, I think I ought to..."

Her voice trailed off very suddenly.

"What?" asked Esofi. Adale seemed to be staring at one of the men, who was dressed in the uniform of a castle footman.

"Audo?" she asked the man, tilting her head to one side. He looked uncomfortable but said nothing. Adale whipped her head around to look at another woman—one of Mistress Abbing's maids. "And you, too! After the last lunar service!"

The maid bit down on her own lip heavily but was silent.

"Adale, what are you talking about?" King Dietrich's voice was heavy with impatience.

"They both kissed the woman!" said Adale triumphantly. King Dietrich stared at her as though she had gone mad, but Esofi's mouth opened very slowly.

Almost two thousand miles away on a slightly raised platform in the center of the great domed entrance hall of the University of Vo Dianene was a statue made of white marble. The statue was life-sized, depicting the Goddess Talcia leaning over a cradle, her lips pressed to the forehead of a sleeping infant. As a child, Esofi had always thought the baby had been Talcia's own, until she was old enough to learn the truth.

One of Esofi's tutors had explained it to her, how the goddess granted magic to newborn babies by kissing them as they slept, and this was where mages came from.

"You saw her?" Esofi whispered, because it was a choice between that and screaming.

Adale looked at her in confusion.

"You *saw* her?"

"I—just—I suppose?" Adale shrugged helplessly.

Esofi wasn't sure why she was crying, but there were tears in her eyes nevertheless. She gripped Adale's arms, desperate and possibly insane. "What did she say to you?!"

"That she wasn't going to kiss me?" Adale seemed to be paralyzed, and she glanced over at her father for help. "I don't... I didn't realize she was anyone important!"

"You all saw her?" demanded Esofi of the gathered Birsgeners. "She visited *everyone except me*?"

"Wait, was that what that was all about?" asked one of the men, catching on at last. "I thought she was just a drunk!"

Esofi released Adale's arms and very slowly crumpled in on herself, her skirts fluffing up to meet her. Anxious hands were upon her at a moment; one of the medics waved a sponge of salted perfume under her nose.

If only her parents weren't on the opposite end of the continent. If only the Silence of the Moon wasn't all but nonexistent in Ioshora. If only there was someone she could talk to besides an apathetic archpriestess and her confused underlings.

"Princess Esofi?" asked Adale. "Are you going to be all right?"

"Let me," said Lexandrie, and Esofi was suddenly aware of her cousin's emerald eyes boring into hers. She brought their faces close together, and when she spoke, it was almost inaudible.

"Talcia has given you a gift," Lexandrie hissed, too quietly for any but Esofi herself to hear. "And yet you are not satisfied because you believed yourself entitled to gaze upon her face? To waste her time with your impertinent questions? In a single grand, unprecedented gesture, she has shown Ieflaria that she favors you, and you still have the gall to pity yourself? You're lucky there's a room full of peasants here, else I would strike some sense into you!"

Esofi looked up at her cousin in shock. She was right, of course—and sounded eerily like Queen Gaelle. The only thing that had been missing from her speech was a comment about her weight. Esofi allowed her cousin to pull her back to her feet, and cleared her throat.

"All citizens who were visited by the goddess must report for training, even if they do not intend to become battlemages. Until construction of a university is complete, we will meet..." Esofi realized she had no idea where she could host the impromptu lessons. "—in the courtyard of the Great Temple of Talcia, I think. The priestesses should not complain."

"They will have little reason to," said King Dietrich.

"Then someone send for the instructors I brought and tell them their services are required," said Esofi. Archmage Eads made a hurrying gesture to his apprentices, and they both bolted from the room, elbowing each other to be first. "All of the newly gifted citizens are to report to the temple immediately. I know you have livelihoods to attend to, but we simply cannot risk one of you losing control of your gift and causing harm to others."

The new mages were quietly herded out by the medics to be taken to the temple by an escort of castle guards.

"We should send out heralds," said Archmage Eads. "There could be more of the newly gifted scattered all across the country. They will need to be brought in or teachers sent to their towns."

"How serious is the prospect of someone losing control?" asked King Dietrich.

"It is difficult to say," admitted Esofi. "Traditionally, mages learn it when they are children. But these people have gone their entire lives with little need for mental discipline. We can only hope they have naturally cultivated the traits that make a good mage. Perhaps it is why they were selected by the goddess."

King Dietrich was quiet for a moment, and Esofi could not guess what he was thinking.

"I would never have dreamed this would happen," she added in a softer voice. "Especially so quickly."

"Nevertheless, we should be able to turn it to our advantage," said Captain Lehmann. "How long does it take for a mage to be fully trained?"

"A lifetime," said Esofi. "It is like being a scholar. You will reach the end of your natural lifespan before you run out of knowledge to acquire. But if you're asking how long before they are battle-ready...I could not say. I only know how our children are trained. I hope an adult will learn more quickly."

"And then if they refuse to fight?" asked Lexandrie sharply. "You heard that woman. How will we convince them to fight dragons when they've spent their entire lives being laborers and craftsmen and shopkeepers? If protecting their own existences won't compel them, what will?"

"Money," said Adale. She looked a bit surprised when everyone stared at her, but then she shrugged. "It's true, isn't it? How much do we pay our soldiers? Offer them that, or maybe even more. Not all of them will accept, but many will."

The doors opened again, and a wave of noise assaulted the healing ward—the sound of a woman screaming. There was a flurry of movement as the healers rushed forward, only to freeze at the sight of Lady Svana, her body awash in emerald magic that lashed out with glittering tendrils.

But Lexandrie was already moving, crimson light gathering at her hands. With just a few smooth motions, Svana and her magic were enclosed in a bubble. Only then did Esofi see that Svana had not come alone—her twin brother was just behind her, more emerald light streaming off him. For a moment, Esofi thought Lexandrie had not completely contained Svana's magic, but then she realized that this magic, though identical in color to Svana's, was Brandt's.

"Oh no," said Adale.

"You must calm yourself," Lexandrie was saying to Svana through the ruby barrier. "Throwing a tantrum will only make it worse because control is dependent on your—*stop screaming or I'll drop this barrier and slap you!*"

Svana fell abruptly silent, probably from sheer surprise, and the emerald light vanished. Lexandrie let the barrier down and Esofi stepped forward, hands out. Svana rushed into her arms, sobbing piteously. Esofi instinctively drew a handkerchief from her pocket and pressed it to Svana's face.

"You're going to be fine," Esofi soothed. "Both of you. You've been given a gift; there's nothing to be afraid of. And I'll help you."

"Brandt," said King Dietrich. "When did you and your sister discover this?"

"It was that servant's fault!" seethed Brandt. "Svana and I sent him to get tea, and it must have been half an hour before he returned. Naturally, we were upset. We've come to expect a higher quality of service."

"So you threw a tantrum and the magic came," said Adale.

Brandt turned on her, eyes full of rage. "I did *not*—" began Brandt, but now the emerald light was back, crackling around his face.

"Adale," said Esofi reproachfully. "Perhaps it would be best not to provoke your cousins until they've learned to control their gifts."

Adale looked like she wanted to object, but in the end, she was silent.

"You need to go to the temple," Esofi told the twins. "That's where we've sent everyone who has suddenly manifested a gift. We're going to teach you control, so you'll be safe."

"You'll come with us, won't you?" warbled Svana.

"Of course I will," soothed Esofi.

Svana seemed to brighten up a little. She sniffed deeply and wiped her eyes on a nearby servant's sleeve.

"Is there any chance we can get it done before sunset?" she asked. "Brandt and I have a ball to host, after all."

A CROWD OF curious citizens had gathered before the steps of the Temple of Talcia, but from the excess of guards that had been posted, it seemed that they were not being allowed on the temple grounds. Esofi supposed it was for the best. As much as the people might want the reassurance of their goddess, it wouldn't be wise to have jittery citizens in the same building as a group of newly blessed adult mages.

Still, as the guards escorted her and the twins from their carriage to the courtyard, Esofi hoped that the archpriestess would come out and address the people soon.

The Rhodian mage instructors were waiting just inside the temple, speaking to each other in low, serious tones. The benches that normally filled the center of the temple had all been moved to one side in order to create a wide-open area. This was where the civilians had gathered.

Esofi approached the mages. They looked about as stunned as Esofi felt. Still, they bowed as she neared, though their eyes were somewhere far away.

"We are ready to begin when the last of the students arrive," explained one of them. "Of course, we don't know when that will be..."

"Then begin now," said Esofi. "There's no point in wasting time."

The instructors called to the gathered Birsgeners to come sit in the cleared area, and Esofi joined them. Brandt and Svana, after some brief complaining about having to sit on the floor, settled down on either side of her.

"The first thing we teach our children is control," began the instructor. Her loud, clear voice rang throughout the temple. "There is no magic in it, only discipline. Moments of uncontrolled emotion can be lethal if you have no training. Once you have a grasp on this, you can choose whether you wish to continue learning from us or return to your lives."

Perhaps it was just her imagination, but Esofi thought the mood in the room lifted a bit.

"Talcia's magic is different from the power granted by other gods," picked up another teacher. "You all know that Adranus gives healing powers to his favored ones, and that Inthi grants a gift with metal and flame to their followers. These gifts fall within the domains of the ones who grant them. But Talcia's primary domain is magic itself. Her magic—your magic—is raw, unrefined power. You've all seen it manifest by now, or you wouldn't be here. If you choose to continue with your studies, we can teach you how to shape this power to your will.

"We will begin with some basic breathing techniques," concluded the second teacher. "As I said before, there is no magic in this. Rather, it is a simple way to calm your mind if you feel your gift threatening to overwhelm you. If you will..."

Esofi closed her eyes and listened to the instructions she hadn't heard since childhood. She remembered sitting out in the gardens with her brothers and sisters, practicing control under their mother's sharp eye. Queen Gaelle hadn't been particularly maternal, but she had been an extremely good motivator.

Her concentration was shattered by the sound of the enormous temple doors opening again. Esofi glanced around to see a new Birsgener stumble in, confused and frightened. Beside her, Svana gave a sharp exhale of irritation.

Unfortunately, that seemed to set the tone for the rest of the day—no sooner did the class get settled when a new student would arrive and need to be caught up. The instructors quickly gave up on trying to impart anything beyond the very basic elements of control, and Esofi couldn't blame them.

Brant and Svana apparently could, though. The twins seemed to have picked up the elements of control with shocking ease and were eager to move on to something more impressive. When Esofi and the instructors urged for caution and patience, the twins argued that they weren't children and shouldn't be held to a child's pace. Esofi had to admit they were right—and besides, surely the reason Talcia had blessed them was so they could join the fight more quickly than children would?

With that in mind, Esofi promised them that they would begin more complex training the next day.

They left the temple a few hours before sunset—the twins were apparently serious about still hosting their ball, despite Esofi assuring them that nobody would blame them for it.

"They say Queen Gaelle of Rhodia can kill people just by looking at them," said Svana dreamily as they crossed the temple courtyard. Bright emerald vines were coiled around her fingertips. "When do we learn how to do that?"

"I...don't think that's true," said Esofi. If it was, she probably would have seen it happen.

Esofi had hoped most of the people waiting outside the temple would have gone away by that point, but it seemed that the crowd had only grown larger over the last few hours. They all fell silent as she approached, clearly expecting a speech.

But before she could think of anything to say, the twins pulled her into the carriage and slammed the door.

ESOFI WAS IN her most elaborate dress yet, a majestic white-and-gold creation that trailed a foot behind her as she walked. Pearls had been embroidered into the lace that covered the bodice, as well as threaded through her hair.

The ballroom was crowded with people, all dressed as opulently as they could get away with, considering the mourning period was not quite over yet. Everyone seemed to be in especially high spirits after the day's events. As soon as Esofi entered, the twins were on either side of her both talking at once. She nodded along and scanned the room, trying to spot Adale. The crown princess was nowhere to be seen. Perhaps she hadn't come? She seemed to dislike her cousins...but she liked parties, didn't she?

Esofi gave a little sigh and glanced back at her ladies. Lisette was already gone. Though, as usual, Esofi had no doubts that the waiting lady could see her. Mireille was drifting toward a group of laughing courtiers, but Lexandrie was still at Esofi's elbow and would remain there unless someone asked her to dance or Esofi did something to shake her off.

A servant was carrying a tray of something that looked like pastries, so Esofi took one. She only managed a single bite before Lexandrie snatched it away from her, but that was such an everyday occurrence that Esofi barely registered it.

Brandt and Svana were now at the center of a circle of people, talking animatedly and occasionally punctuating their sentences with flashes of magic, drawing appreciative noises from everyone.

"They're going to take someone's eyebrows off," Lexandrie murmured in her ear, and there was no missing the eager anticipation in her tone.

Esofi slowly backed away from the crowd and resumed her search, only for someone to take her by the arm.

"Princess Esofi!" cried Queen Saski. "There you are! You look beautiful." Her face was a little redder than usual. "You've done well—we're all so proud to have you."

The ladies with Queen Saski all murmured in agreement.

"Is Crown Princess Adale here?" asked Esofi.

"I haven't seen her yet," said Queen Saski. "But don't worry, she'll turn up at some point."

Esofi nodded and slipped away as soon as Queen Saski was distracted by one of her ladies. Finally, she made her way to the edge of the room and spotted a likely looking servant.

"Do you know where I can find the crown princess?" Esofi asked her.

"I believe she's on the balcony, Your Highness," said the woman.

"The balcony?" repeated Esofi. The servant pointed, and Esofi realized there was indeed a large entryway at the other end of the room, draped with rich velvet curtains. Painstakingly, Esofi made her way through the crowd toward it.

Outside, the air was cool and fresh. The sun rested low on the horizon, and Adale sat alone at a single table, staring at nothing. Esofi cleared her throat, and the crown princess gave a little surprised jump.

"I'm sure you've had an interesting day," said Adale as she approached. The crown princess was wearing a simple, understated gown the color of blackberries. Her usual braid had been pinned up around her head like a crown.

"I suppose I should be grateful that everyone seems to be taking it well," said Esofi, taking the seat across from Adale.

"Of course they are. Why wouldn't they be? Who doesn't love a sign from the gods?" But Esofi didn't miss the twinge of bitterness in Adale's voice.

"Are you disappointed that you were not blessed?" she asked.

"Ha! Me? No. Can you imagine?" That, at least, sounded genuine. Adale seemed to soften a bit. "It is strange to think I saw her twice and had no idea. When people meet with the gods in stories, they're always seven feet tall and glowing with beauty and saying important things. But she just seemed like any other woman."

"Really?" said Esofi.

"Sorry, is that heresy? She did, though. I mean...I did have the feeling she was laughing at me. Most people don't do that—not to my face, anyway." Adale tapped her fingers on the table. "It makes me wonder if I've ever run into other gods without realizing."

"Do you think you might have?"

Adale was quiet, her stare locked on her hands.

"After Albion," she said slowly. "They...before the funeral, they brought him to the Temple of Adranus to prepare the body. There were so many people, priests and healers and I don't even know. Temples are usually so quiet, but this—everyone was shouting. People were crying. Fully trained priests, even! I remember thinking how stupid they were all being. He was already dead. And, and then I noticed there was this man, standing in the corner, writing something in a book. He barely even looked up, and I wondered why he was even there." Adale went silent again. "I'm sorry. That...that made a lot more sense in my head."

"It's all right," said Esofi. "It's... Can I ask how he died?"

Adale looked a little surprised. "You haven't heard?"

"I've been told a few versions of the story," said Esofi. "But I'd like to hear it from someone who was there."

For a moment, Esofi thought she would refuse to answer the question, but Adale spoke at last.

"We were...it was on father's estate at Eandra. We were riding. It was only the two of us... We'd never encountered anything dangerous before." Adale looked down at her hands. "The estate is vast. We go there—we went there every summer since we were old enough to ride and explore the grounds. Every year, we discovered something new. And that year...that year, it was the ravine."

Adale risked a glance back up at Esofi, as if expecting... Esofi wasn't certain what. But whatever Adale saw in her face, it was enough to make her continue.

"It was a stupid way for a prince to die," said Adale. "It was a stupid way for *anyone* to die. I wish I could say I told him not to do it, but I didn't. He had a mare, Wildflower. She was killed with him."

"I am sorry," said Esofi.

"About the horse?" Adale managed a weak smile.

"I'm sure she was a fine horse," Esofi replied seriously.

Rapid footsteps approached, and one of Adale's ladies appeared on the balcony.

"Adale! There you are!" cried the lady. "I'm so *bored*! Let's get out of here."

Esofi looked at the Ieflarian woman in surprise.

"Esofi, this is Lady Brigit," explained Adale. "Brigit—"

"We're all waiting on you, Adale," Brigit proclaimed. "Come on, let's go find a real party."

"What?" asked Esofi, finding her voice at last.

"We're going to sneak out and celebrate properly," explained Brigit. "You could come, if you want, except I suppose you don't want, so—"

"You're going to *leave*?" Esofi asked.

"Believe me, nobody will even notice," said Adale. "Especially with Svana and Brandt showing off."

"Still," began Esofi, but Brigit groaned as though she'd been stabbed.

"There's nothing to do. There's no proper music. I'm going to die of boredom, and it will be on your soul, Adale."

"All right!" snapped Adale. "Gods. Give me an hour."

"You're leaving?" asked Esofi, genuinely disappointed despite the small blasphemy.

"Oh! Brigit's right," said Adale. "You could come along. You might like it. You've never seen the city—not really, I mean. I'm sure the best parties are down by the river..."

"Don't be ridiculous. She's not going to agree," said Brigit in a voice that reminded Esofi of her sisters back home, and perhaps that was why Esofi suddenly rose to her feet.

"Of course I'll come," she said.

SOMEONE MANAGED TO find Esofi an Ieflarian dress that fit well enough. The foreign style was strange on her body, though not uncomfortably so. The dress was in the usual Ieflarian fashion—simple with a short fitted bodice and a long, loose skirt that fell from immediately below the underbust. There were none of the voluminous petticoats that Esofi had become so accustomed to, and she felt oddly naked without them. Still, she thought the style was not without its merits. Movement was free and natural, and it would probably be comfortable during the summer months.

This particular dress looked not unlike the ones worn by the common Birsgener women she had seen. It was pale gray with a white scallop pattern bordering the hem and bodice and a mauve-colored sash around the waist. Someone else found her a short overcoat with long sleeves to wear over it, as the night air was rapidly becoming colder.

Brigit and the other ladies unpinned Esofi's carefully styled hair and rubbed off the majority of her makeup. Finally, after draping a scarf over her head, they declared she was ready.

Esofi owned nightgowns more elaborate than the dress she was wearing now, but at least she would not stand out. Still, she had to fight down feelings of unease as they slipped out of the castle, even at the heart of Adale's group of friends and with the crown princess just beside her, their hands occasionally brushing.

Apparently, there was no shortage of parties to attend that night. The streets were packed with joyous people, laughing and drinking and singing. Someone actually stumbled into Esofi, laughed, and patted her cheek before staggering off again.

"We haven't had a proper sign from the gods in *ages*," explained Lethea. "They're going to be celebrating for days!"

"Oh," said Esofi. She supposed it was preferable to mass hysteria.

The group made their way through the more expensive districts, passing by stone buildings and large, beautifully constructed homes guarded by fences of iron. As they moved through the streets, Esofi noticed that the homes gradually became smaller and less impressive, made of wood rather than stone. The streets were uneven, some dirt rather than paved with stone, and it seemed these areas employed nobody to sweep the streets. In contrast, the celebrating was more boisterous there. Esofi quietly hoped that they were only passing through, but when someone pointed out a tavern, they went inside.

The tavern was warm, uncomfortably so, but Esofi didn't take off her coat. She allowed herself to be pushed onto a long bench at a low table. One of Adale's ladies yelled to the bartenders—she had to yell, considering how loud the music was—and heavy metal tankards were placed in front of them, filled with something frothy.

Esofi glanced around, but nobody seemed to be paying any attention to her. She leaned forward a little and decided that the drink had a distinctly unpleasant scent. It wasn't as if she'd never consumed ale before, though it was admittedly rare that she didn't have wine or juice or even water purified by priestesses of Merla or priests of Eyvindr. She was certain she'd never had ale of this...caliber...before.

She took a bit of foam on the tip of her finger and contemplated it. Not too far away, some of the other patrons of the tavern were bellowing out the words to a song that had a lovely tune but shocking lyrics. People were even dancing, or at least trying to. Esofi watched, oddly entranced by it all. It took her a moment to realize Brigit had been chattering in her ear the entire time.

"—glad we came here instead of staying in that stuffy ballroom?" she was saying. "This is the real Ieflaria, you know. If you want to know what the people really—"

"Brigit," interrupted Adale from Esofi's other side. "I think that man over there wants to dance with you."

Brigit sprang to her feet and hurried toward the man Adale had indicated on the other side of the room. But before Adale could say anything else, another woman took Brigit's place at the bench. Like many of the revelers, her face had been painted with silver stars.

"I love your hair!" the woman shouted, pushing Esofi's scarf aside and putting her hands over Esofi's head. "You did it to look like the princess, didn't you? It's perfect!"

"Um," said Esofi, finding herself suddenly paralyzed.

"Did you have it done just today? I'm going to do the same tomorrow!" The woman released Esofi's head and grabbed at her own ebony tresses instead. "Oh I can't wait! You've even got the color right. Who did you get to do that? Was it the alchemists?"

"Ah," said Esofi. "Yes?"

"I'd love to have one of those big Rhodian dresses, too," rambled the woman. "Don't laugh! I mean it! I know they're silly, but I've already seen seamstresses trying to copy the style. You could make three dresses with the amount of fabric that goes into them! But I don't mind." The woman fell silent, musing. "Though I'm not sure how they get any work done without knocking everything over."

"Nobody works in Rhodia!" shouted Daphene happily, leaning over the table so that she could be part of things. "They just do everything by magic!"

Esofi opened her mouth to object, only to remember that she was supposed to be a native Ieflarian—though only a blind man or the staggeringly intoxicated would actually believe that. Fortunately, there was an abundance of the latter tonight. She fell silent and simply listened to the joyful shouting that floated around her head.

Beside her, Adale very gently put her own hand over Esofi's.

A strange noise filled the air, like a single enormous horn being blown by some herald of the gods. Esofi glanced around, expecting to see someone with a ridiculously oversized musical instrument looking very pleased with themselves.

Instead, what she saw was a room filled with frozen faces. The tavern had gone utterly silent, all the joy and liveliness evaporating like water spilled on a hot road.

"What was that?" Esofi asked.

"The sirens," whispered Lethea.

Adale ran to the door, and Esofi followed her. Just as they reached it, a few terrified people from the street darted inside the tavern. Adale looked upward, scanning the sapphire skyline.

"Do you see—?" began Esofi, just as the sound of leathery wingbeats filled the air. She caught a glimpse of something large and airborne circling the skies before Adale shrieked and slammed the door shut, pressing her body against it like she could possibly hope to hold it shut if the dragon came knocking.

"*IolarTalciaPemeleAdranusEyvindrMerlaInthiDay luueReygmadraEran!*" she cried, naming every major deity on the continent in a single breath. Her face had gone milk white.

"What are we going to do?" screamed Brigit.

"Esofi can kill it!" said Lethea. "She's killed lots of dragons! Haven't you? That's what you said to Theodoar!"

"I—" Esofi looked at Adale helplessly, aware that all eyes were now on her. "Yes, but—but—"

"You don't have to do it!" cried Adale. "The battlemages are right here in the city. They'll get here soon enough! You're not even wearing any armor!"

"Armor?" repeated Esofi blankly.

"And if it burns down the whole street in the meantime?" shouted Brigit. "Or maybe even the whole district?"

Esofi's stomach felt as though it had turned to ice, and was slowly crystalizing outward to her limbs. "I've never fought one alone." But even as she said the words, she knew it wasn't an adequate excuse. There was no adequate excuse, and never would be, because she was going to be the queen of Ieflaria and now she had a responsibility to the city.

All the patrons of the tavern were staring at her.

"I need to get closer," said Esofi. "How can I get onto the wall?"

"There's guard towers every quarter mile," said Brigit.

Esofi reached around the back of her neck and unclasped the necklace she'd been wearing. She removed her earrings next, and then her bracelets, letting them fall to the wooden slats of the tavern's floor. Instinctively, she touched her bodice for any gems that might have been woven into the fabric of her dress, but fortunately this one was plain. Once she was clean of anything that might entice the dragon to tear her limbs off, she went to the door. Adale was still pressed up against it, horror etched in her face.

"I-I'll come with you," declared the crown princess. "Just let me find a sword."

"No," said Esofi. "You would only get in my way."

"Either we're both going or neither of us are," said Adale, but Esofi just shook her head.

"Your parents can't lose you too," she said.

The streets were eerily empty, with only the remains of hastily dropped celebration to prove that the entire population of Birsgen hadn't been wiped out by some plague months ago. The puddles of spilled ale seeped into the hem of her skirt, but she ignored that as she tried to spot the nearest guard tower. Fortunately, they were tall enough that she could see one easily, and the fact that she didn't have the faintest idea of how to navigate the city didn't put her at too much of a disadvantage. As she hurried through the streets, she occasionally caught a glimpse of something small and black hovering just outside her field of vision.

When she finally reached the closest tower, she pulled the heavy wooden door open. There were no guards inside, though the roaring fire and half-eaten meals on the table suggested there had been until very recently. Suddenly thankful for her light Ieflarian dress, Esofi charged up three flights of stairs until she felt the cool night air on her face again.

Gasping heavily, Esofi looked out over the city. In the distance, farther along the wall, she could see the city guards readying a cannon. The dragon swept past them, the gusts of wind from its wingbeats powerful enough to knock the archers' arrows from midair.

Esofi called her magic to her hands, and it came more readily than it had at any point since they'd crossed the border into Ieflaria. Meanwhile, the dragon flared its neck in the way that all dragons did before they flamed. Esofi gritted her teeth and flung her arm out, letting the magic fly like an arrow loosed from a bow. The bolt of light only narrowly avoided hitting the dragon, but it got the creature's attention nevertheless. A massive head swung around to stare in her direction, enormous eyes glittering in the torchlight.

Esofi called more magic up as the dragon launched itself back into the air. She let it flow over her skin, forming a barrier that would protect her from flames and brute-force damage. The dragon was upon her in a moment, and its heavy claws smashed through the stone wall as it landed.

Somehow, Esofi managed to remain on her feet, despite the force of the impact. She forged herself a pair of blades, one for each hand, and lunged for it. The dragon clearly hadn't been expecting to be charged by a creature so tiny, its chest open and undefended. Esofi could practically see the massive heart beating beneath layers of black scales and coiled muscle, and that was where she aimed her blades.

She felt and heard the roar in equal measure and knew she had succeeded. Wasting no time, Esofi turned to run, but she felt something hard and cold snag the nape of her dress. It was one of the dragon's long, curved claws.

I wonder who they'll be sending from home to replace me.

After a moment of resistance, the fabric of the dress tore, sending Esofi sprawling. Her outstretched hands hit the stone, sending pain through her arms up to her shoulders. She lashed out blindly, her magic flailing like a whip, and spun to face the dragon, expecting it to attack—but it did not.

Instead, the dragon gazed at her for a long moment, as if appraising her. Esofi knew she had no excuse for not attacking, but there was something compelling about the way it stared.

It was not the closest she'd ever been to a dragon, but it was the first time she'd been able to truly examine one while it was still alive—though she wasn't sure how much longer it would remain that way. Blood was dripping from the center of its chest, but it continued to simply stare at her.

"Well," said Esofi, unnerved. "Have I got something on my face?"

"*Dro vaq Sibari na?*" rumbled the dragon.

Esofi's mouth fell open. Those had been words—genuine words! And she knew their meaning, more or less. It was the major language of Siabaeld, the continent north of the Silver Isles, where the dragons dwelt.

And this one could speak.

"*Evva—evva vai Sibari,*" said Esofi haltingly. Compared to her mastery of the languages of Thiyra and Ioshora, she had only a rudimentary grasp on it and doubted she'd be able to say anything of worth.

"*I did not wish to die,*" said the dragon. It looked down at the wound Esofi had inflicted. "*I am not ready to see Dia Astera.*"

Esofi had so many questions, but not enough words. "*Then...why?*" she asked, hoping he understood her meaning.

"*Orders,*" said the dragon.

"*Who orders?*"

"*Rvadron.*"

Esofi shook her head blankly at the unfamiliar word.

"*Mother has warned us, but he will not listen,*" continued the dragon mournfully. "*I hope that when he arrives, you pay him the same favor.*"

"*Why do you only speak to me now?*" asked Esofi.

"*You wear Mother's marks,*" said the dragon. "*There, on your back.*"

"Oh," said Esofi, wondering how in the world she could have forgotten. The phases of the moon, ornately decorated and stylized, had been tattooed down her spine in sapphire ink. She had received them as part of her full initiation into the Silence of the Moon. With her dress torn as it was, the marks were now visible. *"Wait! I will call a healer!"*

"I will not betray my Rvadron, even if I could," said the dragon. *"A quick death at your hands is preferable to what he will do if..."* The immense body suddenly shuddered. The blood was coming more quickly now, streaming across the stones. The dragon lowered its head to rest against the ruined wall.

"I am sorry," whispered Esofi. "I'm so sorry."

"You could not know what was never spoken," said the dragon. Its eyes—his eyes—were growing dull. *"Perhaps Dia Astera will be an improvement. I leave this in your hands."*

By the time the guards arrived in a cacophony of iron and shouting, he was already dead.

Esofi was aware they were asking her questions but could do no more than stare blankly. Someone finally grabbed her by the wrists—Captain Lehmann.

"Princess, are you injured?" he demanded. "Can you hear me?"

Esofi shook her head. Then she nodded.

"All right, that's enough," snapped a familiar voice. Esofi turned, as Lisette emerged from the shadow of the tower. She was dressed in hooded leather armor. "The princess needs to return to the castle."

Captain Lehmann released her arms, and Esofi went to Lisette.

"You saw?" asked Esofi.

"I saw," confirmed Lisette. "I heard."

For some reason, this was comforting. "You could have helped."

"I would have if you needed it," said Lisette, unbothered. Esofi started as something touched her back, only to realize that Captain Lehmann was draping his cloak across her shoulders.

"Where is the crown princess?" Esofi asked.

"She's out here too?" Lehmann looked enraged. "Of course. She'll see me cast out of the city yet."

"I left her in a tavern," said Esofi. "With her friends."

"You will find them in the Rabbit District," contributed Lisette. "Now, I need to get the princess back to the castle immediately."

Lehmann barked out a few orders, and Esofi was led down to the ground. There, more guards waited with a pair of Ieflarian mountain ponies for her and Lisette. As they rode through the streets, Esofi could see people beginning to emerge from the buildings warily, still occasionally glancing skyward. But mostly, they stared at her. Esofi spared a moment to wonder how terrible she must look, dress torn practically in two and covered in drying dragon blood.

But that wasn't important, not compared to the fact that the dragon had spoken to her—and in a language of Men, no less. Esofi had been raised to believe that the dragons had lost the ability to speak in ages long past, and none of the dragons she'd encountered had ever challenged the notion until now.

But why? Men had killed so many dragons in the last century. If they could speak, if they could *reason*, it could have all been avoided. But the things the dragon had said made her think that the dragons were actively choosing not to speak.

He trusted me because he realized I was a follower of Talcia. But he saw my magic long before the Silence markings. Why is magic alone not enough?

I need to learn to speak Sibari properly.

They made it back to the castle without incident. Adale was waiting for them just in front of the main entryway, pacing anxiously. When she saw Esofi, she hurried to meet her.

"Are you all right?" cried Adale.

Esofi just nodded.

"You're covered in blood!"

"It's not mine," said Esofi, looking down at her dress.

"Oh," said Adale. "I...I saved your..." She pulled a handful of jewelry from her bag and proffered it to Esofi. Esofi gave a small laugh and passed the jewels to Lisette, who huffed and strode into the castle.

"We're in trouble, aren't we?" asked Esofi, following after her.

"Well, I am," said Adale, rubbing the back of her neck. "I think they'll forgive you, though, since you killed another dragon."

Esofi said nothing. To Adale—to *everyone*—the dragon had just been another roving monster. How in the world could she convince everyone that it was more complicated than that?

"Do you speak Sibari?" asked Esofi abruptly.

"Sibari?" Adale repeated. "A little. It could be better. Why?"

"The dragon spoke to me in Sibari," said Esofi. "Just before he died."

Adale stared at her. "What?"

"He spoke to me," said Esofi. "In Sibari. But he kept saying a word—*Rvadron*. I don't know what—"

"Dragons can't talk." Adale was still frowning. "You told me so yourself."

"This one could!" Esofi gripped a handful of her own hair. It was stained red. "And I think the others can, too. They're just...choosing not to. I swear I'm not mad."

"I don't think you're mad," said Adale. "But I am confused. Why don't the dragons talk to us?"

"It's something to do with Talcia," said Esofi. "And the *Rvadron*. I'm just not sure what. I need to sit down and think, but I'm too exhausted right now."

"The ambassador from Veravin is here with his wife," offered Adale. "You could meet with them tomorrow. Maybe they'll be able to help you."

Esofi rubbed at the blood drying on the side of her face with Lehmann's cloak, knocking it askew. "I just hope they don't think I dreamed the whole thing."

"Even if they do, they can't do anything about it," said Adale. "They're ambassadors, they have to be... What is that?"

"What?"

"The markings on your back... No, don't turn around, I want to see them." Esofi was all too aware of Adale staring on her back. "What are they?"

"It's...difficult to explain," said Esofi.

"I want to see all of it," said Adale, reverently.

Esofi wrapped the cloak around her shoulders again. "Sign the marriage contract, and you shall."

Chapter Six

ADALE

Adale woke with a sense of purpose and a throbbing headache. The festivities had continued into the night after news of Esofi slaying the dragon made it around the city, and she'd seen no reason to go to bed after that. The twins were furious that Adale had managed to steal Esofi away during the ball and had made their displeasure known by spilling wine on her when she'd returned to their party to see if there was any food left.

Adale glanced in the mirror. The previous night's coiled braid had come loose and was now hanging down her back, there was still dried wine sticking to her neck, and she had a cut above her eye where Svana had slashed at her with magic after Adale punched her in the nose. Perhaps a bath was in order.

Every castle, palace, and manor house in the land had a youth blessed with Inthi's gift of flame in its service. Usually no older than ten, the child's sole responsibility was heating water for baths and laundry (and occasionally tea, if someone was feeling particularly impatient). It wasn't a difficult job, and usually tipped well, but it was never permanent. Inevitably, the children would discover a passion for one of Inthi's arts and leave for the workshops, whereupon another blessed child would be brought in as a replacement.

Adale rang for the heater, and they (the blessed of Inthi were almost always neutroi, just as Inthi was) arrived quickly, followed by a trio of maids bearing buckets of water. If—no, *when* Adale was queen, she'd have the metalworkers from Inthi's District put in pipes to run water through the castle, like the ones the emperor had in Xytae.

She took her time with the bath, reflecting on yesterday's events with a surprising sense of satisfaction. Esofi had chosen her over her cousins yet again. Her only true regret was that she'd been useless at helping defeat the dragon. Why had the twins been granted magic instead of Adale? It was fundamentally unfair, decided Adale, conveniently forgetting what her attitude toward the gods had been for the last seventeen years.

Once the water had gone cold, Adale forced herself to dry off, braid her hair, and dress herself. Then she set off in search of the ambassadors from Veravin, the Lord Matvei and Lady Yekarina.

It was still somewhat early, so Adale decided to check the banquet hall first. The ambassadors weren't there, but she paused to eat anyway. When she was finished, she asked the servants if any of them knew where the ambassadors had gone. Someone finally directed her toward one of the sitting rooms.

Lord Matvei and Lady Yekarina were an older couple who spent most of their time with Adale's parents. Like most people from the icy northern continent of Siabaeld, they were quiet, bordering on dour—until they laughed, and then they blazed like a fire. Today, they were alone, sitting across from one another with some incomprehensible board game on the table between them. When Adale entered the room, they both looked up.

"Crown Princess," said Lord Matvei, rising. "Do you need this room?"

"Oh no, not at all," said Adale. "I was actually looking for you."

The couple didn't seem surprised to hear this, but then, they never showed much emotion. Adale closed the door behind herself and took a seat. The two Veravinians continued to watch her, expressionless. She decided not to waste any time.

"Princess Esofi told me something strange last night, just after she slew the dragon that attacked the wall," said Adale. "She said that it spoke to her, in Sibari."

Lord Matvei and Lady Yekarina glanced at one another.

"It said the word *Rvadron* to her," said Adale. "And she thinks it might be important. Do you know what it means?"

"*Rvadron* is a title," said Lord Matvei. "A king, but more than a king. A king over other kings. An emperor. When we speak of Ionnes of Xytae, we also call him *Rvadron*, and Xuefang of Anora is *Rvadrai*—that is the woman's title, and *Rvadat* is for neutroi."

"There was once a *Rvadron* of Siabaeld," added Lady Yekarina. "He ruled all the nations of Siabaeld, the lands that are now called Sterentand and Veravin and Cilva. But no man has held that title in centuries. Now we have only *Zov* and *Ziav*, king and queen, and we are independent from one another."

"Did you know that the dragons can still speak?" asked Adale. "I thought—everyone thought they'd forgotten how."

"They are strange, secretive creatures," said Lady Yekarina. "It makes little difference whether they cannot speak or will not speak, for there is no difference in the quality of silence. Siabaeld remembers a time when they were our allies, but that is past."

"But they don't attack your country, do they?"

"We have the gifts granted by Lady Talcia and Lady Avala," said Lord Matvei, naming the Goddess of Winter who was the Eleventh in Siabaeld. "They know this, and do not trouble us often. And their blood is cold, so the winter makes them sleep. We see nothing of them until midsummer."

It wasn't much, but it was a start. But Adale wasn't ready to bring her findings to Esofi just yet—she had a feeling she could do better. Adale thanked the couple for their help and hurried away, turning the new information over in her head.

The royal library was a place she had only ever visited when she was dragged there by her tutors, but perhaps it held more answers. As she approached the doors, she spared a glance toward the statue of Ethi, the God of Knowledge, just outside. Around the base, a few sticks of incense smoldered, and the offering bowl was half filled with copper coins, sprigs of herbs, and crow feathers. Adale rummaged in her pockets and dropped a few coins into the mix.

Inside, the library was dim and quiet. The front was filled with tables of all sizes, where a few people worked in absolute silence. Farther back was the area where the neutroi librarian-priests shuffled about in their brown robes, repairing old books and muttering to each other. On either side stretched the endless shelves that made up the library collection.

Adale passed the tables and approached the librarians. They all looked confused at the sight of her.

"I need—" began Adale, only to start at how loud her own voice sounded in this place. Trying again, this time in a whisper, she said, "I need information about the dragons."

One of the librarians stepped forward, a pale and smooth-faced neutroi with short black curls. "I will assist you, Crown Princess. Follow me."

Down the dimly lit stacks they went, the librarian seeming to know exactly where to go. Then Adale realized she probably wasn't the first one to ask about the dragons. Her parents or their advisors had surely made the same request before.

After a few minutes of silent walking, the librarian stopped and gestured to a shelf. "Everything from here—" One gloved hand indicated a book bound in faded red leather. "—to *here*—" A thinner tome, this one more folio than book. "—is what we have about dragons." The collection wasn't much, hardly taking up a full shelf. "Beyond this point is wyverns. If you come over to this side, these are the general magical beast books. They might be of use to you if you're just starting out."

Adale looked at the first book, the red one, and began to reach for it, but the librarian stopped her.

"Here, put these on first," they said, withdrawing a pair of silk gloves from somewhere in their robe, identical to the ones all the librarians wore. "Many of these texts are too delicate for bare hands."

Adale put the gloves on and took the book off its shelf. The librarian still looked a bit anxious, though, and added, "If you sit by a window, make sure you don't hold the pages in direct sunlight. And...don't turn down the corners to mark a page. Use this." The librarian reached into their pocket again, this time withdrawing a long white ribbon.

Adale put the ribbon in the book's cover, and the librarian left her at last. She went in search of somewhere to sit. She eventually found a musty-smelling but very soft chair in a little alcove and settled down to read.

The book was titled *Dragons of the North*. The text was old, and many of the words were spelled strangely, though fortunately not so strangely that she couldn't decipher their meaning. The introduction to the book explained that while there were numerous kinds of dragons in existence, the author would be focusing only on the breed that dwelled in Ioshora and Siabaeld and Thiyra, which he called the Greater Northern Dragons.

Adale wondered if there was such a thing as a Lesser Northern Dragon.

It rapidly became apparent that the author of this tome, whoever he was, had been a bit of an eccentric. He'd stalked entire groups ("flights," he'd called them) over mountaintops and across countries, armed with only a notepad and a sketchbook, to study how they interacted with one another and what the stages in their life cycle looked like. The illustrations were interesting to look at, but Adale had a feeling he didn't know any more about the Emperor Dragon than she did. While old, the book had been written long after the dragons had stopped communicating with mankind. Everything this author knew came from observation alone.

He did seem to have his suspicions about dragon intelligence, though. Sprinkled throughout the book were anecdotes that suggested the dragons were far wiser than ordinary beasts. But, he added, the dragons had learned his scent and knew he was observing them. If only he could have watched them in secret, to see how they behaved when they believed no eyes were upon them.

Adale didn't usually do much reading, but this book contained enough tales of risk and danger and aerial dominance fights to keep her awake. Even the disgusting descriptions of molting and the explanations of how a mother dragon would breathe fire onto her egg to keep it warm were actually far more interesting than she'd thought they'd be.

Adale was drawn from the book by the sound of her own stomach growling. Surprised, she looked out the window and saw the sun was directly overhead—she'd spent the entire morning reading.

Adale set the bookmark between the pages and closed the book. She doubted she'd be allowed to take something so old and fragile out of the library, so she returned it to the shelf and decided to go in search of food.

The afternoon meal was already being set out, but Adale found she was having trouble focusing on what was in front of her. Her mind seemed somewhere far away, tracking wild dragons across the north, even while her body sat at the familiar long table. She ate quickly and spoke to nobody—fortunately, nobody tried to speak to her, either. In less than half an hour, she was back at the library, book in hand, her chair still warm.

She finished the rest of the book that day, but despite the wealth of new information about dragons, she still had nothing about the emperor that Esofi's dragon had spoken of. Still, there was an entire shelf of books that she hadn't read yet. Adale resolved to return the following day to see if her luck would be any better.

The next day, she was back again with the rising of the sun, so early that she had to wait outside the doors for the head librarian to arrive and unlock them. This time, she was a little bit more discerning with her selection.

While she thought Esofi would be incredibly impressed if she read every single dragon-related book in the library, she knew they didn't have that kind of time. So after a few more fruitless hours, she decided to approach the librarian who had helped her previously—they had seemed more friendly and approachable than the others.

"Excuse me," whispered Adale. "I need some help."

The librarian looked up from their work and smiled. "Of course, Crown Princess. Are you still looking for dragons?"

"Right. But I don't know if I'm finding what I need here," said Adale. "These books are all fairly recent. I think I probably want something older. Legends, maybe."

The librarian nodded. "I see. You might find more at the Temple of Talcia, then."

"What do you mean?" asked Adale.

"You know that when Inthi forged Inthya it was little more than a molten stone until the other gods filled it with their gifts," said the librarian, citing the creation story that all children knew. "Iolar's gift was mankind. Talcia's was the magical beasts of the wilds, including the dragons."

Adale had always known what Talcia's contribution to the world had been, but she'd never made the connection to the dragons. It seemed wrong that one of the Ten had created such terrible creatures. They were the sort of thing she'd expect from one of those frightening Elven gods, perhaps.

Elves had been banned from all of Ioshora centuries ago, but two had come on behalf of their king in hopes of reopening the border when Adale was very young. None of the regents of Ioshora had chosen to take the elves up on their offer.

Elves didn't look so different from Men; they had two legs, two arms, and one head apiece. But there was such a coldness in their eyes, and the way they walked and gestured reminded Adale of the way a spider zigzagged across the floor when it ran. It was as though, Countess Amala had murmured later, someone had taken a creature with lots of limbs and poured it into a Man's body. Not even the Mer, with their rows and rows of triangular teeth, had ever made Adale feel so cold inside.

But she had seen the carving of the dragon on the courtyard wall when she'd visited the temple with Esofi that day. Perhaps the priestesses did know something— though she wasn't sure if any of them would have the time to help her, considering the influx of new mages. People were starting to come to the city from the surrounding farmland, looking to master their new gifts.

Still, it would impress Esofi and that was the most important thing, or perhaps the most important thing was protecting the city against the emperor and impressing Esofi was only the second most important thing. Adale decided she wouldn't get tangled up in the details. Leaving her waiting ladies behind, she set off for the Temple of Talcia.

The Temple District was never very crowded, even though it was home to the great temples of almost every deity worshipped in Ieflaria. There were a few notable exceptions: the Great Temple of Inthi was located in Inthi's District, where the craftsmen and smiths of Birsgen worked, and the Great Temple of Merla was not in Birsgen at all—it was a hundred miles away on the eastern coast, in Valenleht.

Adale didn't have far to walk because the temples of the Ten were closest to the castle. She traveled slowly, enjoying the morning sunlight and mild breeze. The Temple of Iolar was busiest, with a few elders conversing on the steps—Adale guessed they'd been at the sunrise service and had nothing to do for the rest of the day. A priest argued vehemently with a paladin, and she suppressed a small laugh.

Across the street, dressed in full plate and wielding massive battleaxes, a few priestesses guarded the entryway to the Temple of Reygmadra, Goddess of Warfare. They were stoically ignoring their neighbors, the priestesses of Dayluue, who called hopefully to them as they tended to the roses growing around their own temple.

Adale arrived at the Temple of Talcia soon enough, crossed the courtyard, and entered the sanctum. She knew the students were in the main room where services were usually held, and when she went to the door, she could see the new mages doing...something.

"Can I help you?" asked a sharp voice.

Adale turned, and the priestess who had spoken gave a little start.

"I'm sorry, Crown Princess," she said quickly. "I didn't recognize you. Are you here to observe the training?"

"No," said Adale, casting another glance into the room. Esofi was at the front, smiling and watching one of the instructors explain something to the students. "I was actually hoping I could look at the temple's library."

The priestess gave a nod. "Of course. It is upstairs— let me show you."

Adale let the priestess lead her away from the sanctum and up a flight of stairs that she'd never truly noticed before. The walls were painted with scenes of the night sky that darkened as they ascended.

Upstairs was a wide-open room that looked like it was used for meetings. On both sides of the room were doors, one set plain and ordinary and the other oddly embellished with a familiar pattern. It took her a moment to realize where she knew the design from—it was identical to the tattoo on Esofi's back, or at least, what she'd seen of it.

"What is that?" asked Adale, pointing.

"Oh, it's noth—nothing, Crown Princess," said the priestess, but the lie was clumsy in her mouth. "Please, come this way."

"What's behind those doors?" demanded Adale.

"It's only unused rooms," said the priestess. "Nobody's been in there in an age."

"But the marks on the doors—what do they mean?"

"It's only the phases of the moon," said the priestess, moving toward the opposite doors, the plain ones. "Don't you want to look at the library?"

"Tell me what they mean," said Adale. "That's an order."

The eyes of the priestess hardened, but Adale met her glare evenly.

"It is the mark of the Silence of the Moon," said the priestess at last. "But there is no Silence of the Moon in Ioshora, and so the rooms stand empty."

"What is the Silence of the Moon?" asked Adale.

"It is another way of worshipping Lady Talcia," said the priestess. "Wholly unnecessary—the temple has always been enough."

"If the temple is enough, why is there a room set aside for it in here?" countered Adale.

"The members of the Silence of the Moon dwelt in the wilds. They felt they were closer to Talcia that way. When they were called to Birsgen, the temple allowed them to stay here, out of respect for our shared devotion. But the Great Mother and the archpriestess frequently disagreed, and so the visits were never pleasant." The priestess frowned. "But you have seen their marks before?"

Adale froze.

"You have seen the marks before," repeated the priestess, but this time it wasn't a question. There was a curious, calculating look in her eyes, and Adale could not allow this affront to Esofi's honor to stand.

"I never touched her!" she protested.

"Is that what you think this is about?" said the priestess, eyeing Adale as though she were a particularly foolish child.

"What *is* it about, then?" asked Adale.

The priestess pressed her lips together and shrugged. Adale realized that there was no order she could give that could force the priestess to give a truthful answer, and pelting her with gold coins probably wouldn't get her very far, either. She would have to try negotiating instead.

"If you tell me what you know," said Adale, "I'll tell you what I know about the princess."

The priestess turned away and walked into the next room, gesturing for Adale to follow. As she shut the door behind them, Adale looked around. This was the library, not nearly as expansive as the one in the castle but still full of potential.

"Queen Gaelle of Rhodia is the Great Mother of the Silence of the Moon in Thiyra," said the priestess in a very low voice, drawing Adale's attention back to her. "She thinks that allows her to command the Temple of Talcia. And that may be the case in Rhodia, but it will not be so in Ieflaria. Princess Esofi may have brought magic back to our lands, but we only take orders from our archpriestess and our goddess."

"Esofi isn't like that," protested Adale. "She doesn't want to command the temple! She just wants to protect everyone from the dragons."

The priestess didn't look particularly convinced.

"I mean it," said Adale. "She isn't going to try to undermine you. She's been nothing but respectful of the temple, hasn't she?"

"That means nothing," said the priestess. "You've seen how the Temple of Iolar struggles with the Order of the Sun. The Temple of Talcia is not nearly as strong. We could not withstand that sort of opposition."

"Esofi isn't going to oppose you," insisted Adale. "And even if she was—which she's not—but if she was, she wouldn't have the kind of power that the Order of the Sun does. They've existed here for centuries. It takes time to build up that kind of influence from nothing."

Still, the priestess was silent.

"And besides," Adale went on, "Esofi—she—her mother—they don't... they're nothing alike. Even you can see that."

"Perhaps," granted the priestess, but she still sounded wary. She began to turn away, but Adale realized she had another question.

"Talcia's worship," she said. "Why did Ieflaria abandon it?"

The priestess looked a little surprised at the question. "Why do you think? It is extremely difficult to convince people to worship the one who brought monsters into the world."

"But I thought the dragons only started attacking us after we lost our magic?" pressed Adale. "We were able to fight them before that."

"The people of Ieflaria felt that, if they were pious, there was no reason they should ever need to fight dragons," said the priestess. "Or so it was, back in the days your grandfather ruled. It was a slow thing, at first. Worshippers blamed Talcia when dragons attacked, and so the gifts of magic were not granted as often. Without new mages, the attacks worsened, and so did mistrust of Talcia. It is a cycle that must be broken if we are to survive."

"I think someone already *has* broken it," said Adale.

The priestess tilted her head in a half nod. "Perhaps. But now I will leave you to your reading. Try not to make a mess."

"EMPEROR?" SAID ESOFI.

"That's what they told me," confirmed Adale.

It was just past noon, and Adale had somehow managed to convince Esofi to pause her training so that she could eat while Adale told her of her findings. She also had a pile of notes that she'd written at the temple, and now she sorted through them, trying to find the most useful bits of information.

"Were you able to find anything else about the emperor?" asked Esofi.

"No," said Adale. "But I want to go back and take a closer look. Their library isn't nearly as large as the one we have here, but the books are all more useful. I'm sure if anyone has written something down about the emperor, it's in that temple."

Esofi's shoulders slouched, and she pressed one hand to the side of her face. "I wish I hadn't killed him," she whispered. "He could have told me..."

"Sorry, have you forgotten about the part where he was trying to kill *you*?" Adale interrupted. "If he'd wanted to live, he could have started off by talking, instead of flying around breathing fire at the city watch."

"I know," said Esofi, but she sounded no less miserable. "Still, killing them never troubled me. Why should it have? Farmers don't worry when they eat a chicken. Guardsmen kill wild boars and bears for our protection. The royal huntsman brings carcasses for the castle cook, and he is proud of his work. I was no different from any of them."

"You're right, you're not," said Adale. "There was no cruelty in your heart when you killed them."

"But all this time, I've been wrong. They weren't animals, and I don't even know how many of them I've slaughtered!"

"Esofi, you couldn't have known," said Adale. "In fact, it sounds like they've been doing it on purpose. What did the dragon say to you? He was following orders. Their emperor has forbidden them to speak to us."

"But what could they stand to gain from that?" asked Esofi. "It defies reason."

Adale shrugged. "I don't know either. But I'm going to keep researching."

Esofi gave a small smile. "You know, I never took you for an academic."

"I know. My potential was squandered by tutors who insisted I study boring things," said Adale. "For example. Did you know a dragon will shed its skin once every few years?"

Esofi laughed. "Yes, I did. They're eerie when you find one intact."

"See? And all my tutors wanted to talk about were wars and great-grandparents and what might happen if Emperor Ionnes gets bored of fighting with Masim." Adale leaned back in her chair and sighed heavily. "He's never going to, by the way. And even if he did, Ieflaria is too cold for him."

"You've met him?"

"We went to his wedding... What was it, five years ago now? He spent more time talking about what his troops were doing than anything else, even with Enessa Eusicybr right there. His own mother yelled at him in front of everyone for ignoring his fiancée. The ceremony didn't go on for too long, but the party afterward lasted a week."

"My family was invited, but they decided not to make the trip," said Esofi. "I'd hoped they'd send me with the ambassador so I could meet your family, but my mother didn't want Ionnes thinking we cared about what he was doing."

"Oh, but that would have been fun," said Adale. "There was so much to do, even for children. I think the entire country shut down to celebrate." Adale suddenly looked introspective. "I just had an idea. What if Emperor Ionnes is the dragons' emperor?"

Esofi burst out laughing. "Adale, really!"

"No, I mean it! Everyone knows he wants to take over the world. If he found a way to control the dragons—"

"If he found a way to control the dragons, they would be attacking Masim, not Ieflaria," said Esofi. "Besides, the dragons have been pretending to be animals for centuries now. He's barely thirty."

"All right, yes, but what if it's a family tradition, passed down through the generations in secret?"

"No, Adale," said Esofi, gently but firmly. "Emperor Ionnes is not the emperor that the dragon was referring to. His family could not have kept that kind of power secret for so long."

Adale made a disappointed sound. "It can never be the easy answer, can it?"

"I'm afraid not," said Esofi with a wry smile.

Adale suddenly realized that she had actually been enjoying herself. "Where are the twins?"

"Oh, they didn't tell you? They've gone home," said Esofi.

Adale missed her mouth with her drink. "They... what?"

"Oh, not forever. They promised they would be back in less than a week. They said they had to retrieve something."

"From Valenleht?"

"I think so. Or...no! They said they were going to visit their mother's estate. But they wouldn't say why." Esofi smiled. "It's a surprise."

Examining her feelings, Adale realized that she was oddly unbothered by this. Let the twins have their schemes. She was doing important work.

"Is it safe for them to be running around with almost no training?" asked Adale.

"I think so," said Esofi. "I hope so. They're both very talented. As long as they don't lose their tempers, they're easily the best in the class."

THE LITTLE LIBRARY kept by the Temple of Talcia was not as organized as the Royal Library. There was evidence that someone, at some point, had attempted to group the books by subject. But it seemed the collection had been neglected for a very long time, and so Adale was left with no choice but to examine each book individually.

She was not so disciplined that she could simply begin with the first book on the highest shelf and work her way across. At first, Adale selected the books with interesting spines and bright colors, with dyed leather covers and gilt edges. Unfortunately, most of those texts were too modern to be of any great use, and had nothing at all to do with dragons.

Never one for moderation, Adale decided instead to look for the oldest, rattiest, crumbliest pile of parchment and dust that she could find. She found a likely looking tome after a few minutes, sliding it off the shelf carefully. A thin stream of dust fell to the floor in its wake.

Adale brought the book to the table and opened the cover, which made a terrible cracking sound and immediately detached itself from the book's spine. She looked around hastily but was alone. Perhaps the priestesses would believe that it had been broken before Adale got to it. Perhaps they would not notice at all.

As she turned to the first page, Adale's heart sank when she realized she could not read the title—it was in some ancient dialect that she had never seen before. But the illustration just below it was promising. It was a drawing of a dragon, silhouetted against the moon.

Adale chewed her lower lip, thinking. Perhaps one of the court historians could make sense of it, or one of the priests at the library. But for some reason, the thought was unappealing. They were probably all doing whatever it was they did for her parents that kept Ieflaria running. She shouldn't bother them with her silly whims...

It's not silly. It could be the key to defeating the dragons.

Or it could be nothing but useless nonsense.

The sound of footsteps ascending the stairs outside made Adale turn a few more pages rapidly, hoping they were enough to hide the detached cover. As the door opened, she arranged her face into what she hoped was an innocently neutral expression.

But it was not a blue-robed priestess that stood in the doorway. Instead, it was Esofi, her skirts threatening to catch on the doorframe.

"Princess?" asked Adale. "What are you doing up here?"

Esofi glanced around the little library. "I could ask you the same thing. Are you still searching for information?"

"Yes," Adale said. "Are you surprised?"

Esofi gave a very small smile. "A little, though perhaps that is unfair of me—I do apologize."

"How is the training coming along?" Adale asked. "Or have you grown tired of it already?"

"I needed to rest my mind," admitted Esofi. "But our newly blessed students have excellent instructors and so I do not think my absence will be any terrible loss. And I was curious—I have never been in this area of the temple before."

She had to have seen the doors, the ones with the carvings that matched the markings inked onto her back. But Esofi said nothing about them, and so Adale did not raise the subject.

"Well," said Adale, "I think this book looks promising, but I can't read it—the dialect is too old. I was just wondering if it was worth troubling the court historians over."

Esofi came over to look at the open page. She squinted at the words for a long moment and then shook her head in defeat, her curls bouncing with the movement.

"I could not begin to read that," she said.

"Some of it looks a little familiar, here and there," said Adale. "See...I think that word is egg. The... egg...something, is hatched, maybe?...and is...I don't know that word...the dragon—ahh, that word is dragon, maybe that will help..."

"Would it help if I took dictation for you?" asked Esofi.

"Maybe," said Adale. "I think it's easier to understand if I stop thinking and just say the sounds as they appear." She began to flip through the pages again. "But that will take an age. Stop me if you see anything that might have to do with the emperor."

To Adale's surprise, Esofi took a seat and settled in to help. But even with the princess's help, it was several hours before they happened upon anything particularly interesting.

Despite her expectations, Adale had fallen into a sort of rhythm with the old dialect. It was strange in her mouth, but she was able to determine the meaning of most of the words. With her eyes half focused and mouth relaxed, she found she could make her way through entire pages—far more than she'd ever believed possible when she'd first opened the book.

"...in that time, Mother granted the blessings of the Moon to her children alone. The foremost of her blessing was the...glittering...darkness that can be shaped to all things. But Mother saw her...husband's children, and she was...compelled. She began to share her blessing with the...hatchlings of Man, and the Men grew to love her and call her Mother just as we always had..." Adale looked at Esofi. Esofi stared back at her, clearly thinking the same thoughts.

"Was this book written by a dragon?" asked Esofi.

Adale looked down at the book before her and imagined a dragon dipping the end of his silver claw into an enormous inkwell, trying to fit words onto tiny pages.

"He must have had a Man to perform the transcription," said Adale, though the image that this conjured up was only slightly less ridiculous.

Esofi rested the side of her face in one hand and stared at nothing.

"Have you ever seen a dragon use magic before?" asked Adale.

Esofi shook her head. "A dragon with Talcia's magic would be a terrible thing to see," she said. "But they are one of her finest creations, and I can believe it was once so. It just seems odd that she would stop granting them magic."

"Unless she's angry at them," pointed out Adale. "They're going out and acting like dumb beasts and getting themselves killed. Maybe she decided they don't deserve magic anymore. Like she did here in Ieflaria when her worship started dying out."

Adale and Esofi returned to the palace for the evening meal. Adale was satisfied with all that she had accomplished so far, but she wondered if Esofi felt the same way. Did she blame Adale for taking her attention away from the newly blessed mages, or had she enjoyed poring over the old book?

But Adale was back the very next morning, ready to find more information that might be valuable. While Esofi continued to instruct the new-blessed Ieflarians, Adale continued to work her way through the ancient text. It was not as much fun without Esofi there to discuss her ideas with, but she was determined not to bother the princess until she found something important.

And so it was not until well past noon that Adale happened upon something that prompted her to run downstairs and drag Esofi away from her training. So great was her excitement that she practically pushed the princess up the stairs, though this was made difficult by the size and density of Esofi's skirts. Fortunately, Esofi was not offended and laughed as Adale tried and failed to hurry her along.

Once upstairs, Adale rushed over to the table and grabbed the book before Esofi even had a chance to seat herself.

"Here, listen!" Adale said. She looked up to make sure Esofi was paying attention and then began to read. "The Flight is led by the Most Blessed. The Most Blessed is...selected by Mother...as the most powerful and...devoted...and is given..." Adale frowned. "The scent? The scent which compels obedience and unity among the Flight in times of danger."

"Compels?" repeated Esofi.

"I think the emperor's control over the other dragons is more powerful than him just outranking them," Adale explained. "It seems like he might actually be able to force them to follow his orders. I don't know if it's magic or something simpler. But it almost reminds me of bees in a swarm, obeying their queen."

Esofi looked thoughtful. "Did you see any mention of a way to break his influence?"

"No. But I think the emperor isn't supposed to go around controlling everyone all the time. From what the book says, I think it's because dragons aren't good at working as a community. They're too independent. But if a bigger threat comes along, they need to work together. That's where the emperor comes in."

"So the emperor has decided that mankind is a threat they must band together against," mused Esofi. "I only wish I knew why."

"Perhaps we can take one hostage and ask," said Adale, prompting Esofi to laugh again. But Adale secretly wondered if she could do it, if she had her friends and some soldiers and some battlemages along to aid in the capture.

Esofi must have sensed her thoughts, because she said, "I do not believe your parents would appreciate you taking such a risk. Nor would I."

"Don't say that, there's still the twins." Adale smiled. "One way or another, you will have your wedding."

"It's not about the wedding," said Esofi. "I do not wish to see you killed, for your own sake."

Adale waved her hand to cover her discomfort. "Never mind that."

"But I do mind," Esofi said. "Very much. Or do you intend to blame yourself forever?"

"Everyone else does," retorted Adale. "Why shouldn't I?"

"They do not," Esofi insisted, leaning forward. "And even if they did, they are wrong. It was an accident. It is not as though you murdered him for the crown."

Adale could not help but laugh, and it seemed to free some of the darkness in her heart. "Yes, fortunately there was no question of that."

"You are trying, Adale," said Esofi. "Perhaps you will never be what Albion was, but you are not Albion. Nor are you the careless young woman I met two weeks ago. I hope you know how much that means to me—and to Ieflaria."

Adale hoped her cheeks weren't too red. Desperate to turn the subject away from herself, she said, "You're different too, you know."

"Am I?" Esofi laughed in surprise. "How so?"

"When you first arrived in Ieflaria, you would never have slipped away from a ball to dance in a tavern with foreign peasants," Adale reminded her.

"I didn't dance," said Esofi quietly.

"You might have if the dragon hadn't attacked so soon. My point stands." Adale crossed her arms. "Come on. Aren't you hungry? Let's go find something to eat."

Accompanied by a few guards, Adale and Esofi returned to the palace. The air was mild, and the sun was not too strong, and so they decided to take tea on the green, in the place where they first met.

"The priestesses have had a trying week," observed Esofi. "But I like to think they are grateful for the excitement. The Temple of Talcia seemed to be a rather quiet place before I arrived."

"You make the priestesses anxious," Adale admitted. "Or I suppose I should say, your mother does."

Esofi's eyes were bright with curiosity. "What do they say?" She set down her teacup.

"Don't look at me like that. I don't know much," said Adale, raising her hands in a gesture of surrender. "They're just afraid that you...or the Silence of the Moon...will undermine them. Like the Order of the Sun and the Temple of Iolar."

Esofi sighed. "I do not wish to undermine the temple, but I understand their apprehension."

"What is the Silence of the Moon?" asked Adale. "That is...if you're allowed to tell me."

Esofi rested her arms on the table. "It is not a secret, exactly, but there was something very mysterious and elite about it in Rhodia. My mother liked to claim it was the way Talcia preferred to be worshipped, away from temples and civilization. I do not know if she was correct, but I do know that it was pleasant to spend time away from the palace."

"What did you do, once you were out in the wilderness?" asked Adale.

Esofi was quiet for a moment, thinking of her answer.

"To an observer, it might not seem that we were worshipping at all. But when Talcia's children worship her, they do not cease their daily lives. They have no rituals or songs, and they build no temples or statues. They simply...live. To exist in her wilderness, with our thoughts focused on her love, is no different from how a gryphon or a roc worships." She smiled up at Adale. "You would probably find it terribly boring."

"Maybe," said Adale. "But I find temples boring as well. I am only having difficulty picturing you barefoot in a forest somewhere."

Esofi laughed. "It is too cold in Rhodia to go barefoot. Besides, it was not as rustic as you are thinking—the court would not tolerate that. We had great camps prepared so that we could return to luxury when the desire struck us."

"That sounds like cheating to my ears," teased Adale.

"Perhaps! But we are still Men, for all that my mother wishes she were a dragon. I think Talcia cannot fault us for the traits her husband gave us." Esofi looked thoughtful, pensive. "I would like to see the Ieflarian wilderness. Particularly your northern lands. I am sure they are beautiful."

"Perhaps you should arrange for a tour of the kingdom to follow your wedding," suggested Adale. "I'm sure nobody could object to it—dragons are no match against you, and the people would love to see more of you."

Esofi smiled. "Perhaps." But before either of them could say any more, they were interrupted by a breathless maid.

"My ladies," she whispered, chest heaving. "Forgive my intrusion, but Lady Svana and Lord Brandt have returned to the city. And they have brought with them—"

"Their manners?" muttered Adale.

"Shh, be polite," said Esofi. She smiled at the maid. "Where are they?"

"On their way," said the maid, pointing across the green. "You can already see everyone gathering."

She was correct. Where there had been nothing but empty lawn and a few idle courtiers five minutes ago was now a swiftly growing crowd of onlookers who spoke excitedly to one another.

Adale frowned and got up. "What's this all about?" But nobody seemed to have an answer for her. Then from up ahead, there was a shout of "Step aside!" and the crowd parted, revealing the twins. Something large and white walked between them, shying away from every sudden movement.

"What do they have?" asked Adale. "A horse?" Though she'd never seen a horse of such a color before. Its coat was painfully white, like harsh winter sunlight gleaming over fresh snow, and it was slender and long-legged, like the horses of Masim and the southern lands, but there was something not precisely right about the shape of it. Something quite unlike a horse at all.

Before Adale could inspect her thoughts more closely, before she could consider the cloven hooves or strange tuft of hair at the animal's chin or the leonine tail that swept from side to side anxiously—before she could do any of that, the creature turned its head to the side and Adale saw, for the first time, the long and gleaming crystal horn that protruded from its forehead.

Esofi spilled her tea down the front of her dress.

Immediately, two different maids lunged forward with cloths to soak up the liquid, but Esofi seemed not to notice them. She moved toward the twins as if in a trance, and her hands very gently went to the unicorn's face.

"It has lived on our mother's lands for as long as anyone can remember," Brandt was saying in a loud voice. "But we are the only ones who have managed to catch it."

"You must tell me how you did it," said Esofi.

"I sang to it," said Svana smugly. A rope of glittering green magic was wrapped around the unicorn's neck and clasped firmly in her hands. Adale almost bit through her own cheek while Esofi continued to exclaim over the creature.

"Do you like it?" asked Brandt at last.

"I *love* it," said Esofi. She looked up. "This is so thoughtful. I shall never forget this. But..." She gazed at the unicorn, and it gazed back at her, almost...knowingly?

"But?" prompted Svana.

"Unicorns are magical creatures of the wild," said Esofi gently. "To confine one in a city would be wrong. You must bring him back to your mother's estate."

"Then you reject the gift?" asked Brandt.

"This moment is gift enough," said Esofi. She lowered her hands. "Promise me you'll have him sent home?"

The twins glanced at each other, speaking with their hands and eyebrows in that way they sometimes did.

"Of course, Princess," said Brandt, inclining his head slightly. "Of course."

THE MOURNING PERIOD was over, and Adale found that she was actually looking forward to the engagement ball. Esofi had not made a formal announcement regarding her choice—that would be done at the ball itself—but confidence filled Adale with a warm glow.

Her mother seemed to agree, and it was with the contributions of what felt like every lady in the castle that Adale prepared for the evening. At the end of it, she was dressed in a gown made of midnight-blue silk with her braids coiled around her head in a complicated and somewhat uncomfortable way that nevertheless perfectly suited the tiara her mother had given her as a gift that same evening. Everything was new, from her shoes to her stockings to her gloves, and when she looked in the mirror, Adale thought that perhaps she wouldn't be the worst queen in Ieflarian history.

She thanked her mother and her ladies profusely for their help and set off to find Lethea and Daphene, who had disappeared at some point during the application of face powder. As she walked down the familiar hallways, she noted to herself that the shoes weren't nearly as uncomfortable as she'd assumed they would be.

The halls were so quiet it was almost eerie, but that didn't dampen her spirits. Adale smiled to herself, wondering what trouble her friends had gotten themselves into this time and hoping it wouldn't require any running or lifting to get them out of it—the dress was so delicate, she was afraid it might tear if someone looked at it too hard.

She didn't notice the tendril of emerald light snaking around her foot until it slammed her to the ground.

When her vision cleared, all she could see were the twins sneering down at her.

"What are you doing?" shrieked Adale.

The twins both rolled their eyes in unison. "What do you *think* we're doing, Adale?" retorted Svana. "We don't know why you're insisting upon carrying out this farce. You'd only doom Ieflaria if you married the princess."

Adale tried to get up, but the vines were multiplying, binding her hands and legs together. "So this is your plan?" she cried, outraged. "You think that Esofi won't hear about how you assaulted the crown princess? I'll tell her that—"

"By all means, inform Princess Esofi," said Svana cheerfully. "I'm sure she'll believe that your loving cousins committed treason and risked exile to lock you in a room for twelve hours when it's far more likely that you just changed your mind about the marriage and ran off to get drunk in some horrible tavern."

A tendril wrapped itself around her head and across her mouth, cutting off any reply Adale might have given. The twins moved quickly, dragging Adale along the ground until they reached a familiar door—Albion's old room. Brandt pulled out a key, unlocked the door, and they shoved Adale inside. With a sudden slam of the door, Adale was alone in darkness with only the faintly glowing light of emerald magic.

Adale tried to scream, but the vine in her mouth didn't allow for it. She wriggled desperately, but the magical vines weren't like rope. They couldn't be broken or loosened at all.

Of course. Of course. Why had she thought the twins would just accept the loss gracefully? She had been so distracted by the dragons and so certain of Esofi's affections that she'd completely failed to keep an eye on the twins, despite knowing perfectly well that they were more of a threat than ever before with their new magical abilities.

Thank you, Talcia, thought Adale. Why would the goddess give her gifts to those two? Why would any deity? Had Talcia known this would happen?

Had Talcia *wanted* it to happen?

Sod her. I don't care what she wants. If Talcia wanted Esofi to marry one of the twins, she could come to Birsgen and tell her in person. Until then, Adale wasn't going to give up. She paused to think and catch her breath. Iron was known to interfere with magic. Was there anything in the room made of iron? Adale focused, trying to pick out something helpful in the darkness.

But now the emerald vines were dissipating; either the twins had lifted the magic or it had worn off. The moment she was free, Adale scrambled to her feet and rushed to the door, only to find it was locked. She yanked at the handle and kicked repeatedly, but it was useless—this room had once belonged to the crown prince, and the door could withstand a siege.

"Hey!" yelled Adale. "Anybody! I'm locked in!"

But even as she shouted, she knew it was useless. Everyone from the lowest serving maid to the captain of the royal guard would be at the betrothal already.

Adale pressed her back to the door and slowly slid to the ground.

"Damn it," she whispered. Svana was right—Esofi would never believe her side of the story, not with anything less than a Truthsayer to confirm her words, and Truthsayers were rarer than diamonds. It would take months for the Order of the Sun to locate one and then months for him to travel to Birsgen. By then, it would be too late.

Still, she forced herself to get up and go to the window, stumbling in the darkness. Someone had removed the expensive glass and boarded it up, so Adale spent a few useless minutes cracking her nails as she tried to wrench the wood free before giving up.

Adale went to the especially dark corner of the room where she knew the fireplace was. Fortunately, it wasn't boarded up, and after a minute of scrabbling around, she felt a handful of sad little coals within. It took a bit of searching to find the flint, but she managed to get the coals lit. They barely gave more light than the magical vines had, but it was enough to locate a candle and set it aglow.

After taking a moment to congratulate herself, Adale went over to Albion's desk to see if there was anything useful inside. It was filled with all sorts of things—nobody had cleaned it out during the mourning period. Something colorful caught Adale's eye.

It was a miniature portrait of a tiny blonde baby girl with ribbons and curls in a lacy white dress. She was standing, so Adale supposed she was old enough to walk on her own but had no idea how old the child might be beyond that. Adale picked it up to find there was a whole stack of portraits underneath, each no larger than her hand.

The next portrait was the same girl but looking a little older, in another delicate dress. The next one featured the girl again, but now she looked like she was about the same age as the castle pages. Adale set the picture aside and went to the next—the same girl but now the age of a temple acolyte, draped in pearls. Now she was familiar enough that Adale finally recognized her.

Esofi.

It made sense, of course, but for some reason, Adale suddenly felt oddly hollow, as though Albion had led a secret life that she'd never known about. She set the portraits aside and looked at the papers underneath.

Letters. Addressed to Albion and written in delicate curling handwriting. Adale turned the first paper over and skimmed to the end, where it was signed with Esofi's name.

Adale felt her heart lurch.

A thousand unwanted emotions rushed through her as she stared at the signature, followed by the odd feeling that perhaps she oughtn't read the letter, perhaps it was none of her business what Esofi had had to say to Albion. The words had been meant for him, not for her, and Albion would have shared it with her if it had been any of Adale's concern.

But before she could make a decision, the doorknob rattled, and Adale dropped the paper.

"Is someone there?" shouted Adale, rushing forward just as the door swung open. Lisette stood in the doorway, lockpicks still in her hands. Peering over her shoulder was Mireille, who beamed widely when she saw Adale.

"You!" said Adale. "How did you—?"

"Quickly," said Lisette.

Chapter Seven

ESOFI

Esofi stood in the doorway to the ballroom, her ladies on either side, listening to the sound of her heartbeat and the soft rustling of her own petticoats. The room before her was already filled with laughing, glittering Ieflarians and curious foreigners, all waiting to hear her decision. In one corner, she could see Squire Ilbert and a few footmen guarding the marriage contract, which was complete save for the blank space where the name of Esofi's betrothed would be filled in after she announced her choice.

"Princess Esofi of Rhodia," announced the herald, his voice echoing across the ballroom. "Lady Lexandrie of Fialia, Lady Lisette of Diativa, and Lady Mireille of Aelora."

The room fell silent, and Esofi felt a bit light-headed. She was certainly used to being stared at by hundreds of people; it had been a regular aspect of her childhood, after all. But rarely was she the unequivocal center of attention. Attention would rest on her for a moment, then move on to her siblings before usually settling on her parents.

But now, everyone was watching her, and her alone.

Esofi stepped forward into the ballroom, a soft smile on her face. The servants had outdone themselves tonight. Everything gleamed, from the wooden floors to the candlesticks. It seemed every archway had been decorated with early roses and every plinth held an enormous gold vase that was near to bursting with flowers.

Esofi's dress was pale-golden silk intricately embroidered with patterns of flowers in bloom. The upper skirt parted in the front, revealing the second layer of ivory skirts beneath it. The sleeves were held against her skin until they reached her elbow and exploded into three separate layers of loose ruffles, similar to the ruffles around her neckline. The bodice of the dress was brocade and had been sewn with tiny diamonds.

Around her neck, she wore a triple-stranded pearl necklace set with an enormous yellow sapphire. Her earrings and bracelets were pearls as well, and although it was impossible to see them, her shoes had also been sewn with pearls. Her ladies had styled her hair as usual, but this time instead of ribbons or flowers, she wore a small golden filigree tiara.

She was immediately approached by some Ieflarian nobles, but she barely heard their compliments. She scanned the room, but it seemed neither the twins nor Adale had arrived yet.

Carriages had been arriving for the past few days, bringing guests from all across Ieflaria and even beyond. It was equal parts betrothal ceremony and celebration of the end of the mourning period. Even an olive-skinned couple with crowns resting in their dark hair were at the center of another crowd—King Marcius and Queen Isabetta of Vesolda.

King Dietrich and Queen Saski were the next to enter, bringing the room to a hush. They were both accompanied by their retinues, but Adale was not with them. Esofi waited to see if she would be announced afterward, but the next party to arrive were from Armoth, one of Ieflaria's western fiefs.

Esofi approached Saski once the initial wave of people greeting the queen had drifted on to other things.

Saski's face brightened when she saw Esofi. "Oh, my dear, you look so lovely. I'd hug you, but I'm afraid for your dress. I can't tell you how happy I am to have you here."

"Thank you," said Esofi. "Have you seen Adale yet?"

"She's not here yet?" asked Saski.

Esofi shook her head.

"But she left before I did. How...odd. I'm sure she'll be here any moment, then. She was extremely eager for tonight, you know."

Esofi nodded and told herself that she was being silly. Adale wanted her. She hadn't spent hours researching the dragons solely out of a sense of responsibility—had she?

No, Esofi told herself. Not Adale.

The twins were the next to arrive, in matching outfits of pale-blue silk. They completely ignored everybody except Esofi, attaching themselves to her sides as they always did, their hands stroking her arms softly as they spoke. Perhaps they were feeling less homesick than usual, because they seemed to be in especially good spirits that night, with no complaints about the food or the decorations or the servants.

As the bell chimed six, the musicians began to play and people began wandering toward the floor to dance. Esofi stared at them, unseeing, while Mireille and Lisette whispered fiercely to one another behind her back.

"Wouldn't you like to dance?" asked Brandt, holding out one hand to her. Some of Adale's friends were already on the floor, and so she took his hand and allowed him to lead her in a dance—only to slip out of his grasp at the first spin-and-release and intercept Lady Daphene before she could return to her own partner.

She'd half expected Daphene to be offended, but Adale's lady seemed to find the whole thing funny.

"Have you seen Adale tonight?" Esofi asked over the music.

"What? You mean she's not here yet?" cried Daphene. She was an extremely good dancer, if not a bit too exuberant, spinning Esofi so quickly that she was afraid she'd be sick. "That's impossible!"

"You didn't come in with her?" asked Esofi, halting in her steps, a sick dread rising in her stomach.

"We thought she'd left without us," said Daphene. "Really, I mean it—we thought she'd left us behind because she couldn't wait to see you. Wait, I'll sort this out." Daphene gestured to her friends to come nearer, creating an obstruction on the dance floor but not seeming to care. "Does anyone know where Adale is?"

Within a minute, it was clear that nobody did.

"Perhaps she wants to make an entrance," suggested Lady Brigit. "Something really stupid, you know? She's been simmering ever since the twins brought in that unicorn. I bet she's off trying to find someone to sell her a winged horse."

This got some laughter from the group, as winged horses were known to be even rarer than unicorns, at least on the continent of Ioshora. Esofi couldn't find it within herself to smile, though. She merely nodded and walked off the dance floor.

Fortunately, one side of the ballroom was lined with chairs for exhausted dancers. Unfortunately, before she could make it over there, she was pulled aside by Queen Saski.

"You haven't seen my daughter yet, have you?" Saski's tone was light, as if the question was no more than a casual inquiry, but Esofi knew the truth. Adale still hadn't arrived and probably never would.

Esofi didn't trust herself to look the other woman in the face, so instead, she stared at a point just over Saski's shoulder.

"I'm sure she will be here soon enough," said Esofi, pulling out of the queen's grip. Then she accepted a glass of wine from a servant, who gave her a humiliatingly pitying look, and went to go sit down.

Across the crowded ballroom, King Dietrich was now giving harsh orders to a pair of castle guards, his hands clenched into furious fists. He pointed out of the room and then at the floor in front of him. The guards saluted and rushed out of the ballroom. Esofi had a sinking feeling that she knew what they had been sent to retrieve.

But she didn't want that. She didn't want to marry someone who needed to be dragged before her. She wanted to go over to King Dietrich and tell him not to bother, but for some reason, the idea of approaching him filled her with sadness.

Then, quite suddenly, she was aware of someone sitting down next to her. She turned to look, expecting to see one of the twins but instead found herself staring down at a little girl in a rather large dress of blue brocade. The style was unusual, and Esofi couldn't quite place it.

"Hello," said the little girl calmly. "Do your feet hurt?"

"Ah..." said Esofi. "No? Do yours?"

"Not anymore!" said the little girl brightly and extended her feet out beneath her dress, showing off bare white stockings. Esofi couldn't help but laugh.

"You're Esofi," the little girl said. "Right? Either you're Esofi, or she is." The girl pointed across the room at Lexandrie, the only one of the waiting ladies that Esofi hadn't lost track of.

"No, you're right, I'm Esofi," she assured the child. "What's your name?"

"Vita." From Vesolda, then. That explained the odd dress. "Which one are you going to marry? *Mada* says you get to pick."

"I don't know," said Esofi honestly. "I thought I would marry the crown princess. But...she hasn't come. I think she might have changed her mind."

"She's stupid, then," announced Vita.

Esofi tried not to laugh. "We mustn't talk that way about the crown princess."

Vita pressed her lips together and shifted them back and forth in an odd way. "Are you going to tell them you can't decide?"

"I can't," said Esofi. "I've already waited too long."

"Tell them to bring you someone else," suggested Vita. "Someone new."

That was certainly an idea. But while she had a feeling nobody would question her not marrying Adale, she knew that she didn't have a good reason for rejecting the twins.

"I'm afraid it's too late for that," said Esofi sadly.

"Esofi!" cried Brandt. She looked up to find the young man standing before her. "There you are—I was afraid I'd lost you! Are you all right?"

"I'm fine," said Esofi, but her tone was brittle and fake. "I just needed to rest my feet. I'm sorry."

Brandt took the seat on Esofi's other side and gave a very quiet sigh.

"You must be so disappointed," he said, leaning in close to her. "But that's just how she is. Even you've realized that by now. My cousin means well, she truly does, but she's always had difficulty with carrying out her duties..."

Esofi gave a small nod and lurched to her feet. "Excuse me. I'm going to get some air."

The balcony wasn't too crowded, and Esofi ignored any and all attempts that the Ieflarians made to bring her into their conversations. She rested her palms on the cool stone of the railing and stared down at the brightly lit city below.

Nothing has changed. I will still be the queen of Ieflaria. That's all that matters.

All she had to do was pick one of the twins.

Esofi paused to consider this. They were so alike, the twins, and never one without the other. It was almost difficult for her to separate them in her mind. Regardless of which twin she married, the other would never be far away.

Svana had a voice that could coax a unicorn close enough to be captured and had woven flowers through Esofi's hair. Brandt was quiet and gentle, just how she'd always imagined Albion to be, and she knew she would always feel safe with him.

She didn't know. How could she choose? Esofi was half inclined to toss a coin and leave the choice to fate.

Or perhaps...perhaps being the queen of Ieflaria wasn't her destiny at all. She lifted her gaze to the horizon, in the direction of Valenleht, Ieflaria's largest and most important port city. Beyond it lay the ocean and, past that, the rest of Inthya.

Lexandrie wouldn't follow her, but Mireille and Lisette might. She could go to Anora and meet the Empress Xuefang at the Pearl Court, and they could all sip pale, bitter tea and laugh over her tale, because surely the journey would put enough distance between herself and Ieflaria to make the entire thing funny. Or perhaps she would go to the Burning Isles and be adopted by a tribe of bronze-skinned warriors who would spear sharks out of the ocean and teach her the names of gods she'd never heard of before. Or maybe she could go to the Elven lands and become a governess for the Elf King's children. She would teach them how to eat with a fork so they could finally be accepted into the lands of Men.

She would save that one for last, though.

On the far horizon, movement caught her eye—a flock of birds wheeling toward the city. She wondered vaguely what sort of birds flew so near to dusk. Some odd Ieflarian species, perhaps...

Some large Ieflarian species...

Her eyes widened, and realization struck at the same moment that the first siren began to wail.

Esofi spun around and dashed into the ballroom. Already, people were beginning to panic. She grabbed her skirts and forced her way to the exit, which was actually quite difficult since it seemed like everyone else was going in the opposite direction, trying to get to the balcony so they could gawk uselessly at the sky.

Finally, Esofi was free of the crowd. She ran from the ballroom and raced down the halls of the castle, past frantic servants and shouting guards. As she went, she unclasped her necklace and let it fall to the floor. It was followed by her bracelets and then her earrings, leaving a trail of gems in her wake. She paused a moment to rip the diamonds from her bodice, and that was when Captain Henris caught up with her.

They stared at each other for a long minute, and then Esofi tore the last gemstone from her dress and let it fall to the floor, never once breaking his gaze.

"Princess, there are at least twenty dragons out there!" yelled Henris. "I can't let you—"

Esofi felt like perhaps she had been possessed by a demon as she threw a wave of sparkling pink light at the man who had been her loyal protector, slamming him against the wall. Henris looked dazed as Esofi sprinted past him, her mind already on the upcoming battle, all too glad to shed her thoughts of weddings and disappointments.

Nobody else tried to stop her, and Esofi made her way down to the stables, knowing a horse was her only chance of getting to the city wall before the dragons overran Birsgen. There were no hostlers around to aid her, and so Esofi went to the stalls, hoping perhaps one of the horses might still be saddled.

To her great surprise, the unoccupied stall next to Adale's horse now had a resident in the unicorn that the twins had brought. It was clearly agitated, swinging its head from side to side and gazing up toward the sky.

It knows. Then inspiration struck.

"Do you speak Ieflarian?" she asked, looking the unicorn full in the face.

The unicorn did not respond, though it did stare at her.

"*Dro vaq Sibari na?*" she asked. "*Dei vou Rhodiania? Vaai Dassauvi? Vod Eska?* I've already spoken to a dragon; I know you can understand me!"

The unicorn merely continued to stare, though now it seemed like it might be amused. Or perhaps that was merely wishful thinking.

"I know you're angry at us, and you've a right to be," said Esofi. "But there is an emperor coming to kill us all. If he succeeds, you'll never get back home. I think I can stop him. But I need to get down to the city wall. If you help me, I will..." Esofi wondered what in the world she could offer a unicorn. "I will make it illegal to trap your kind for any reason. You will be safe from Men for the rest of your..." Esofi hesitated again. "How long do unicorns live for?"

The unicorn laughed, Esofi was certain of it, exhaling rapidly through his nose and making an amused sound from within his chest. Esofi gave an incredulous laugh as well.

"Very well," it said. No, not it—he. The unicorn had a sonorous voice that matched his beautiful form. "But only because I know the dragons would not grant me that same protection or even the protections I have now."

Esofi felt a little ill. "You mean they'd eat you?"

"My poor mad cousins? Yes," said the unicorn. "Now let me out of here. It smells of sorrow."

Esofi threw the latch and wrenched the stall open. "Thank you. And I am sorry—I didn't realize you weren't an animal. I didn't realize the dragons weren't either until only a few days ago."

The unicorn turned his head to one side as if inspecting her. "One spoke to you? But that is forbidden."

"Why?" asked Esofi. "Why aren't you allowed to speak to us? It would make things so much easier if you could! You could have representatives at King Dietrich's court, and nobody would mistakenly harm you."

"You misunderstand," said the unicorn. "I am not forbidden to speak. I merely choose not to. The dragons, however...the emperor has ordered their silence. It makes them easier to control. He would face more opposition if his subjects began to think of Men as their equals."

Esofi had a thousand questions, but the unicorn knelt with his front legs so Esofi could easily climb on to his back. It was difficult with her heavy and complicated skirts, but the unicorn rose easily, as though she weighed nothing.

"What should I hold on to?" asked Esofi, who had never even considered riding without a bridle or saddle.

"Not my mane, you'll tear at it," said the unicorn. "Put your arms around my neck. And try not to dig in your heels."

Esofi did as he said, leaning forward against his warm neck. His horn gleamed in the fading light like a naked blade, a fearsome weapon. Yet he had not used it to escape the twins or attack any of the Ieflarians.

The unicorn broke into a canter, and Esofi clung tighter. He was far, far faster than any horse and rounded the side of the castle within minutes. Then, with the road down into the Temple District in sight, he broke into a gallop.

He could have outrun any horse in the world easily. Esofi had wanted to ask him more questions on the way to the city wall, but now she was afraid that she'd bite off her own tongue if she attempted to speak. She gritted her teeth together and watched the assorted districts of Birsgen fly past, occasionally catching a glimpse of an openmouthed citizen staring at her in wonder.

As they drew nearer, Esofi could see the dragons hovering in the sky, occasionally swooping down to engage with the guardsmen that had flooded out to defend the wall. But they weren't truly attacking, not yet.

The unicorn skidded to a halt. "I will go no further. I do not wish for them to catch my scent."

Esofi slid off his back and tumbled to the ground. Her legs felt strange and numb, and she couldn't feel her fingers at all, but now she was close enough that the shouting of the city guards, followed by echoing roars, reached her.

"Which one is the emperor?" Esofi asked.

"I could not guess, Princess." The unicorn lowered his head for a moment. "I wish you well."

"Thank you," said Esofi solemnly. "And I meant what I said—if I live, I will make this country safe for your kind."

"I know," said the unicorn. "I would not have carried you if you had lied."

Esofi felt her eyes widen. "You are a Truthsayer? But that is Iolar's magic! You are a creature of Talcia."

"And you are a creature of Iolar who carries Talcia's magic," the unicorn reasoned. "Is that any different?"

Esofi swallowed. "Thank you," she said again.

The unicorn nodded at her before turning and galloping back in the direction of the castle.

Esofi hurried the rest of the way to the wall. But as she neared, she realized it wasn't just city guards who had gathered. There were some priestesses of Reygmadra in their heavy plate armor and some paladins from the Order of the Sun in their chain mail and even some artisans from Inthi's District, their hands alight with orange flames. A few bright spots of color caught her eye, and she thought her own battlemages stood among them, having somehow beaten her frantic dash to the wall.

It was only when she emerged from the guard tower and onto the wall that she realized that they were not Rhodians at all—they were her own students, the newly gifted Ieflarians.

They gathered around her when they caught sight of her, hope and joy in their faces. They weren't ready. They barely knew how to maintain a shield. They would be slaughtered! Esofi felt sick as she searched for a diplomatic way to order them back to the dubious protection of the temple. Talcia could not have meant them to die so soon and so terribly. It was unthinkable.

"Who is in charge here?" asked Esofi. There was a moment of silence as all the gathered Birsgeners looked around at one another.

"You are, Princess," said one of the neutroi of Inthi at last.

Esofi had been afraid of that. "Where is Captain Lehmann?"

"We sent for him," said one of the guardsmen. "He was at the betrothal. He's on his way, I'm sure of it, along with the battlemages."

"We're battlemages!" objected one of Esofi's students, a skinny woman who had worked as a shepherdess just outside the city before she'd been gifted.

"The true battlemages, then," the guardsman retorted dismissively. Esofi's students seemed prepared to show their disagreement, but she cut them off before the infighting could begin.

"That's enough!" she said. "I'm going to try to talk to the emperor. Nobody attack, not for any reason, unless the dragons try to overtake the wall. Even if the emperor engages me, do not attack. I want to try to end this without any loss of life. Does everyone understand?"

"You cannot reason with a dragon," said someone close by. Esofi looked around to find who had spoken, and a woman wielding a massive war hammer stepped forward. It took a moment for Esofi to recognize her—Gertra, Archpriestess of Reygmadra.

Esofi decided that there was no time to attempt to justify her actions. She walked toward the edge of the wall, gazing up at the dragons. "If I am killed," she announced to nobody in particular, "please tell King Dietrich and

Queen Saski that I am deeply sorry for the inconvenience and that my sister Esybele might be willing to come replace me if they ask very nicely."

Then she leapt from the wall, bringing her magic to her hands to slow her descent enough to land safely on the long grass outside the city. She looked to the sky, but none of the dragons approached her. They seemed to be waiting for something, though Esofi could not guess what. But she knew what would get their attention.

Turning her attention to the fields before her, she called her magic to her hands. She took a few steps back to examine her canvas and began to sear designs into the long grass. She had done this as a child, as a game, admiring the glowing pink marks until they faded away or the gardeners spotted her and began screaming.

Now, she drew a luminous pink waxing crescent, followed by a half moon, then a full moon, and another half moon, this one waning, and then finally a waning crescent. It was a simpler version of the tattoo on her back, and she knew she had been successful even before she was completely finished with it, because one of the dragons, the largest one, was moving quickly and purposefully through the sky.

It dropped to the ground before her, the force of its landing almost knocking her over. Esofi kept her balance, though, and stepped forward to address it.

"Are you the emperor?" she asked.

The dragon said nothing.

"Please answer me," said Esofi, allowing her magic to envelope her skin in a protective barrier. "I know you can speak."

The dragon opened his mouth and roared. Esofi screamed back at it, a wordless sound of pain and outrage.

As the last of the sound died away, the dragon made a sound that sounded not unlike a laugh. He lowered his massive body onto all four of his legs and brought his head down to Esofi's height.

"So, you are the one who has been killing my scouts," he rumbled. "I was told to fear you, but you're no different from any other Man."

"This is my city," said Esofi, surprising herself with how strong and clear her voice was. "This is my country. You and your soldiers will leave."

The emperor threw back his head and bellowed out a laugh that echoed across the sky. "Little hairless rat! You think to order me? I rule the skies and all below!"

"Be reasonable," said Esofi. "Talcia has already warned you—"

The emperor struck her lightly, almost casually. Esofi went flying back into the stone city wall. Fortunately, the magical shield over her skin buffered her from all but the worst of injuries. She staggered forward, and a few shattered pieces of rock fell from her shoulders and onto the street. Up on the wall, the Ieflarians shouted, but she gestured at them to hold their positions.

"You speak of things you do not understand!" roared the emperor. "When Mother sees how easily I have destroyed her new favorite, then she will finally realize how pathetic your kind is!"

"Is that why you hate us?" asked Esofi. "You think she favors Men over dragons?"

"She has favored Men for generations!" the emperor shouted in her face, the force of it knocking the last of the pins from her hair. "She has given blessings to your kind and revoked them from us!"

"The people of Ieflaria have learned that Talcia revokes her gifts when her will is ignored," said Esofi. "But if you repent, she will forgive you, and you will find yourself blessed again. I can help you in this, if you will listen to me."

The emperor laughed like an earthquake. "Men have nothing to teach dragons. I would be offended if I were not so entertained. When I finally rule over your lands, I will remember you with fondness."

Esofi raised her head to the sky where the other dragons were waiting. She wondered if they believed in the emperor's promise to eradicate mankind or if they were as unwilling as the one that had spoken to her.

But before she could ask any more questions, the emperor flared his neck in the way that signaled he was about to flame. He opened his mouth wide, and the scent emerged of noxious fumes gathering in his throat that would explode into magical fire in only a moment. She leapt aside just in time as the flames struck the wall behind her spot of just a moment ago.

From the skies above came a symphony of shrieks and roars, and the dragons began to move en masse toward the city wall. Esofi gritted her teeth together in despair, but she knew she had to trust the people of Ieflaria to protect their own city. Her opponent at the moment was the emperor.

He swung his head to follow Esofi's progress across the field, keeping his body lowered to the ground so that she could not pierce his heart as she had so many dragons before. Deprived of her most familiar attack, Esofi was forced to think creatively. A dragon's back was heavily armored, but the wings were comparatively delicate.

She called her magic to her hands again, releasing it from her palms just enough to propel herself a few meters off the ground, just high enough to leap onto the emperor's back. Her hands grasped at his coarse scales, which jutted enough from his body for her to pull herself up. He made a sound of outrage and twisted his body around, trying to shake her free, but Esofi found his enormous wing joint and wrapped her hands around it tightly. Her head slammed against his body as he flailed, but she forced herself to hold on.

Finally, perhaps deciding that this course of action was undignified, the emperor spread his wings and launched himself into the sky, spiraling up toward the distant clouds. The delicate warmth of springtime quickly gave way to icy cold, and her hands began to slip. Esofi allowed her magic to race up her arms and gather in her hands, forming a pair of long daggers that manifested half within the emperor's body. Instead of giving them hilts, she made the ends into gauntlets that clamped tightly around her wrists, leaving no chance that they would slip from her aching hands.

The emperor's flight faltered as the sudden pain in his wing registered. His other wing still beat, but he was losing altitude. Esofi poured more of her magic into the blades, lengthening them and digging them deeper into the emperor's wing.

He crashed to the ground inelegantly, rolling over onto his back. Esofi barely had time to dismiss the daggers and leap to safety. Pain shot through her leg as she connected with the ground, but she ignored it.

"You little *worm*!" he bellowed, blood trickling from his wing. "I will tear your disgusting fleshy hide off, one strip at a time!"

"Come try it, then," said Esofi, gasping heavily. She spared a glance back toward the city, where the Birsgeners on the wall were engaged in a hundred battles with the other dragons. She could not tell who was winning and did not have time to evaluate their situation.

The emperor flared his neck, preparing to breathe his flames once more. But this time, Esofi knew what she had to do. She called her magic to her hands once more and let it propel her forward and directly toward him.

Alight with rage and magic in equal measures and lacking a more sophisticated plan of action, Esofi leapt into the emperor's mouth.

A cry of shock emerged from his throat, and for a moment, all she could see was her own magic glinting off sharp teeth and rippling muscles. At the back of his mouth was a cavernous pit of darkness, and that was what Esofi hurled herself toward now. The stench was unbearable, but she hardly had time to consider it before the world burst into painful flames that tore at her protective shield and singed her hair.

Esofi did not waste her energy by screaming. Instead, she struggled to move on the soft, squishy interior of the emperor's mouth. It was his tongue, she realized, and he was curling it, trying to force her into the path of his teeth.

Using her magic, Esofi forged a lance and plunged it into the base of the dragon's mouth, clinging desperately to it. For just a moment, she caught a glimpse of the night sky as the emperor opened his mouth and bellowed in pain. His head tilted upward, so she released the lance and rolled toward the back of his throat.

As she moved, she pulled in every drop of magic she had, sinking it back into her core. Even the shield was sapped away as she funneled it into its source at the heart of her very self. She drew it in, in, in, compressing it down as tightly as she could force it to go. It trembled within her, straining to go somewhere, burning and aching—

Finally, when Esofi could stand the pain no longer, she released it.

A single wave of light seared her vision for the briefest of moments before the blackness overtook her.

ESOFI OPENED HER eyes and gazed into a sapphire sky studded with stars, clear and bright and oddly close. Her head was rested against soft leaves, and she sat upright carefully, surprised by the lack of pain in her body.

Birsgen was gone, instead replaced by quiet wilderness.

She looked around, shaking dry leaves and flower petals from her hair. In front of her were the smoldering remains of a campfire, and just beyond that was a woman, dressed in the heavy, coarse clothing of a hunter, who poked at the embers with a long stick.

"What happened?" Esofi murmured.

"You threw yourself into the emperor's mouth," said the woman. "An unorthodox strategy, to be sure."

"I'm dead, then," said Esofi, with the distinct feeling that she'd been cheated of something. Tears of bitter disappointment sprang to her eyes as she thought of everything she hadn't had time to accomplish.

"No, Princess," said the woman patiently, and it was in that moment that Esofi knew that she was no more a woman than the unicorn had been a horse. "You are not dead. You are, however, badly injured. But you will live. I only brought you here because I thought it was time we talked."

Realization struck Esofi, and it was like waking from a dream. "I—I'm sorry!" she babbled. "I had no idea—I only—I was taught they were animals, wild animals, nobody knew, none of us knew—they would have destroyed us if we hadn't—"

Talcia raised a hand, and Esofi immediately fell silent. "I know. How quickly things have changed. Once they were wise and noble. But now you have surpassed them. It has been...difficult." Talcia looked away. "In the beginning, I only granted my gifts to my children. But the races of Men were so numerous and so full of love. So many voices, so many prayers. I could not resist you for long."

"And the dragons became too wild even for you?" guessed Esofi.

Talcia's mouth lifted in a brief smile. "Never. Impossible. Make no mistake—it is not wildness I object to. It is evil. Cruelty. Greed. Gluttony. That is why I revoked my gifts." Her gaze met Esofi's, and Esofi had the sudden sickening sensation that she was falling through the sky. But then the goddess blinked, and she was back in her body again.

"Perhaps it was my own error," said Talcia quietly. "To make them so magnificent that they believed themselves infallible."

"The emperor was angry," said Esofi. "He was jealous. He believed you loved Men more than the dragons."

Talcia laughed, and for a moment, Esofi caught a glimpse of her the way the dragons saw her: an enormous dragon, twice as large as the emperor had been, with gleaming ebony scales and burning yellow eyes.

"Men?" she asked. "With your carefully tended fields and elaborate palaces? With ribbons in your hair and bread in your hearths? You play in the woods for an hour and think you know wildness. You have touched it with a fingertip, nothing more. Still—" She seemed thoughtful. "I will see to him next. I expect we have much to discuss. But you need to focus your worries upon the living."

"What do you want from me?" asked Esofi.

"The very thing you want from yourself," said Talcia. "You mean to be the queen of Ieflaria, do you not?"

"I don't know if that's going to happen," Esofi admitted sadly.

"No?" Talcia tilted her head. "After everything, you have lost your desire?"

"It's not that simple," said Esofi. "I would have chosen Adale. But it would seem she has not chosen me."

"How very mistaken you are," said Talcia.

Esofi opened her mouth to ask what she meant, but the goddess interrupted.

"You doubt me? I think not. Now *go*. And I don't want to see you here again for another sixty years."

She awoke.

ESOFI OPENED HER eyes again. Stony pain filled every inch of her body, and her vision was blurry. Something was dripping into her eyes.

"Princess?" Esofi was just able to make out a woman's shape before her. "Can you hear me, Esofi?"

Esofi nodded, but the motion sent a wave of nausea shuddering through her body. "The emp—" she began, but her mouth was filled with dry ash, and the rest of her words were lost to a hacking cough.

"We need a healer!" bellowed Adale to someone she could not see. "Don't move, please, please! We'll get this all cleared in a moment!"

Already, some of the heavy pain was being lifted away from her, but there was still something pressing uncomfortably against her stomach and arms.

"The emperor?" Esofi asked again, wiping her face on her shoulder, but it did no good—her shoulder was similarly stained. Someone—a healer wearing the robes of a priest of Adranus—wiped at her face with a cloth, and Esofi could see again. She realized the heavy things crushing her body were not stones, but enormous chunks of dragon flesh, and it was blood that stained her from head to toe.

Adale was still gazing down at her, face streaked with tears, her arms wrapped around Esofi's shoulders.

"I'm so sorry," whispered the crown princess in a broken voice. "Gods, Esofi, I'm such a fool. I'm so sorry."

"Why?" asked Esofi, still feeling a little dazed.

"Princess!" That was Captain Henris. "Thank the gods! Are you all right?" He entered her field of vision, and the toll that the battle had taken on him was obvious. His robes were torn and singed, and his face was covered in dry ash.

"What happened to the emperor?" Esofi insisted.

"There," said Henris, gesturing to something large and unmoving a few hundred yards away. It looked like the emperor, but its head was missing, blown off at the neck. "The others fled when it fell."

It was only the fact that she had refrained from eating anything all day long that saved Esofi from retching onto the street.

"You jumped on its back," said Adale in an oddly shaky tone, "and then you leapt into its mouth! Are you *mad*? I thought you were going to die just like Albion—" Her words turned into a pained wail, and she began to sob.

Suddenly feeling deeply guilty but unable to free her arms, Esofi pressed her cheek to Adale's shoulder. "I'm sorry I worried you," she whispered.

Adale rested one hand behind Esofi's head, stroking her wet hair, but said nothing more.

"I'm sorry. And I probably smell terrible, too."

Adale burst into laughter even as she continued to cry. "You're right, you do!" She sobbed. "Also, you—you, you have no eyebrows!"

Esofi laughed, but for some reason, it came out as tears.

Adale looked alarmed. "No, I didn't mean it like that! No, you're still beautiful. They'll grow back. Please don't cry!"

Esofi laughed again, and this time, it came out right, except the tears were still there so she simply laughed and cried at the same time, utterly drained and completely overwhelmed. But Adale looked distinctly relieved.

"Crown Princess," said Captain Henris, "I understand that this is a difficult time for you, but perhaps you can get out of the way so we can free Princess Esofi?"

Adale reluctantly released Esofi, and she rested her head on the grass.

"I'm sorry I struck you," Esofi informed Henris. "I was...upset."

Henris gave an incredulous laugh. "I'd forgotten about that. It seems a lifetime ago. Think nothing of it."

"No," said Esofi. "I shouldn't have done it. It was wrong. Please accept my apology."

"Princess," said Henris, "I sincerely—after everything—you cannot believe I am angry because you had a moment of..." He seemed unable to find the word he sought. "Besides, if you hadn't done it, you might not have been able to defeat the emperor before he overran the city."

"Please," Esofi pleaded more softly, and something in Henris's face seemed to change.

"Very well," he said. "I accept your apology. All is forgiven. Now let's get the rest of these...pieces...off you."

"Yes, please," said Esofi. "Something is pressing into my ribs terribly."

The last of the "pieces," as Henris put it, were removed from her body quickly, but the odd pain remained. There were a few quiet gasps, and Esofi looked down, expecting to see something terrible, like her own entrails. But instead, nestled against her chest, wrapped in her arms, was something very warm and very large, with a curved shell that gleamed faintly in the twilight.

"What is *that*?" asked Adale.

"It's an egg," said Esofi, with the sudden suspicion that she might be dreaming. "It's a dragon egg."

Others were beginning to gather around, murmuring soft words of amazement.

"Where did it come from?" asked one of the Rhodian battlemages.

"Was it *inside* the dragon?" asked another. "Was it a...female?"

"No," said Esofi. "No. It was...a gift. From Talcia." Understanding blossomed in her. "Adale, we need to get married before it hatches, or it will be a bastard. I won't have that."

Adale looked alarmed. "I—what?"

Oh. She had forgotten. Esofi hugged the egg to her chest. "Never mind, I—never mind. Where are the twins?"

"Are you—no! No! No! No!" Adale looked around desperately. "No. No. No, no, no. I need to explain, it's not what it looked like. Your own ladies can vouch for me. They're the ones who broke me out!"

"Broke you out?" repeated Esofi. The healers set to work, but Esofi ignored them, even when they did something to her leg that set her entire body aflame with pain.

"The twins locked me in Albion's room so I would miss the betrothal," said Adale.

"Don't be ridiculous—" began Esofi.

"I know you won't believe me, so I'm not going to try to convince you," Adale interrupted. "Ask Lisette or Mireille. They're the ones who managed to find me. They got me out just in time, as the sirens went off."

"But the twins—" Esofi protested weakly.

"They're awful!" cried Adale. "They always have been! Ask *anyone*! You've seen how they treat people! That's why I didn't suggest them to you the night before Theodoar tried to duel you! I didn't want you trapped in a marriage with one of them!"

Esofi looked up at Adale, torn between wanting and not wanting to believe her. From nearby came the sound of someone clearing her throat, and Esofi turned to look. Lisette was standing just beside Captain Lehmann, dressed in a tattered ball gown with a distinctly unhappy expression on her face.

"Lisette," said Esofi weakly. "She's lying, isn't she? Isn't she?"

Lisette merely pressed her lips together. "Do focus on recovering, Princess. I need you to get well enough for me to be able to slap you."

THE FIRST DAY of summer was bright and beautiful, and so they spread a blanket on the lawn and took their lunch there. Adale's friends were particularly rowdy, shouting and singing and drinking (and encouraging Mireille to join in) while Lexandrie sat at a table a few meters away and turned her nose up at them. She had been in a terrible mood ever since the twins had been politely but firmly escorted back to Valenleht, which surprised Esofi to no end.

Usually, Lisette would watch such events from some shadowy alcove or rooftop, but she seemed to have decided the time for subtlety was past. She sat at the table next to Lexandrie, quietly cleaning a hand crossbow.

At the center of it all was Esofi and Adale, the former heavily bruised and bandaged, and both extremely happy. Settled just between them was a lump of fabric the size of a housecat. It was left undisturbed, for now.

As the last song drew to a close, a long shadow fell over the blanket. "I see I've missed all the fun," said a quiet voice, prompting everyone to look up.

"Theodoar!" cried Adale in delight, springing to her feet. She wrapped her arms around him in a hug and lifted him a few inches off the ground.

"Hello," said Esofi mildly.

Theodoar blanched. "Princess. You look...ah..."

"She looks *beautiful*," insisted Adale.

"The healers say all this nonsense can come off in another week," said Esofi, gesturing to her leg. "And the bruises will fade soon enough. Honestly, I feel fine. I know I look terrible—no, don't object, I own a mirror—but really, I'll be perfect in time for the wedding."

"Yes, and we'll all shave our eyebrows in solidarity," said Lady Brigit from somewhere in the back. Esofi picked up a half-eaten pastry and hurled it at Brigit's face. The shrieks of laughter told her that she'd struck her target, and Theodoar gradually began to smile.

"Come sit down," said Adale. "You haven't met Carinth!"

"Carinth?" repeated Theodoar, but at that very moment, Adale untangled the lump of blankets, revealing a very, very small dragon with blue-gray scales and enormous golden eyes.

Theodoar gave a yelp and leapt back in shock.

"He hatched two weeks ago," said Esofi. "I was hoping he would wait until after the wedding, but I'm not as upset as I thought I would be. Look how big he is already. It's incredible. When he first hatched, I could hold him in one hand."

Theodoar continued to stare, his lips moving but no sound emerging.

"Give him a gold coin and he'll be your friend," suggested Adale.

Esofi smacked her shoulder. "Stop telling people that! We're trying not to encourage hoarding behavior!"

Theodoar sat down beside them, offering one hand to the baby dragon. Carinth sniffed it curiously, his little tail waving back and forth.

"What are you going to do with it? Him?" he asked.

"Well, I don't think anyone is going to accept him as our heir," mused Adale. "So hopefully he'll be an ambassador. Of course, with me as a mother, he might turn out to be a wandering minstrel instead. But here's hoping."

"You as a mother?" repeated Theodoar with a laugh. He reached out to stroke Carinth's back, and the baby dragon arched his spine into the touch, like a cat might.

"Don't laugh! Who was the one who knew we had to put the egg on the fire? That was me!" Adale looked extremely proud of herself. "I read it in a book. And I *also* knew that we had to grind his food up into chunks, and that he's not going to start flying until he's about a year old, and plenty of other things that I've forgotten now, but I can look them up again because I know how libraries work."

"You're so smart," said Esofi affectionately, pressing a kiss to Adale's cheek. Adale wrapped her arms around Esofi and kissed her on the lips for so long that her friends began to whistle. Eventually Carinth broke them apart by climbing onto Esofi's neck and sticking his long tongue into her ear, making her shriek.

"Rude!" Esofi scolded Carinth as they broke apart. She picked him up and held him out so that she could examine him fully. "We don't lick people's ears. That's disgusting."

Carinth didn't seem too upset by the admonishment and wriggled free of her hands in order to chase after a butterfly, his tiny winglets unfurling occasionally in the soft breeze.

Esofi sighed. "He's hopeless. We've ruined him already. What am I going to tell Talcia? Don't answer that," she added as Adale opened her mouth to speak. "I can't listen to any more of your blasphemy."

"Well, I have unfortunate news," said Adale. "Just about every other thing I say is blasphemy."

"Well, can you at least try to space them out?" asked Esofi. "One per month, perhaps? Instead of six in the course of a single afternoon?"

Adale laughed. "I'll see what I can do." She laced their fingers together and kissed the back of Esofi's palm. "Because I am madly in love with you."

Esofi smiled. "So am I. Now, please go fetch our son before he falls into the well again."

About the Author

Effie is a librarian living in the Philadelphia area with her cat. She writes science fiction and fantasy.

Email: effiecalvin@gmail.com

Twitter: www.twitter.com/effiecalvin

Website: www.effiecalvin.com

Also Available from NineStar Press

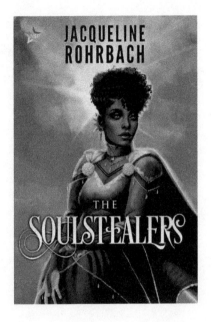

Connect with NineStar Press

www.ninestarpress.com

www.facebook.com/ninestarpress

www.facebook.com/groups/NineStarNiche

www.twitter.com/ninestarpress

www.tumblr.com/blog/ninestarpress